PRAISE FOR MARIELITOS, BALSEROS AND OTHER EXILES

"In a smorgasbord of narrative styles, through a melding Spanish and English, we learn about the Cuban exiles' dreams, fears, failures and victories, and about loves lost and gained—each tale a journey towards the truth of immigrant life in contemporary America; a life which they alternately curse and celebrate. Cecilia Rodríguez Milanés' stories are a family fiesta, to which the reader has received a special invitation."—**Judith Ortiz Cofer**, author of *The Latin Deli and The Meaning of Consuelo*

"It's as if Cecilia Rodríguez Milanés had spent her entire life hiding in the closets, kitchens and bedrooms of all the Cubans I once knew in Little Havana, Hialeah and 'La Saguecera,' taking notes. In this delicious book of short stories, nothing escapes her unflinching eye: she understands how Cubans love, cook, argue, work, dream, cry, and die. She gets the Cuban soul."—**Mirta Ojito**, author of *Finding Mañana*

"Cecilia Rodríguez Milanés is a gifted story teller, and these wonderful stories add a powerful and lasting voice to the cannon of Exile literature. I salute this publication and its writer by drinking a strong Mojito and lighting up my best Partagas cigar."—**Virgil Suarez**, author of *The Cutter*, *Latin Jazz*, and *90 Miles: Selected and New Poems*.

"There is wisdom, humor and hurt in these engaging stories of exile. Rodríguez Milanés draws you into the world of her characters and makes you feel for and with them. An impressive debut!—**Gustavo Pérez-Firmat**, author of *Life on the Hyphen: The Cuban-American Way*

MARIELITOS, BALSEROS AND OTHER EXILES

MARIELITOS, BALSEROS AND OTHER EXILES

CECILIA RODRÍGUEZ MILANÉS

BROOKLYN, NEW YORK

"Muchacha (After Jamaica)" was first published in *The Albany Review*. Abuela Marielita," was first published in *Iguana Dreams: New Latino Fiction* edited by Virgil Suarez and Delia Poey (HarperCollins). "Failed Secrets" was first published online at Damselfly Press. "The Fresh Boys," was first published in *Linden Lane Magazine*. "A Matter of Opinion," was first published in *Emrys*.

Printed in the United States of America
10 9 8 7 6 5 4 3 2 1

Ig Publishing
178 Clinton Avenue
Brooklyn, NY 11205
www.igpub.com

Library of Congress Cataloging-in-Publication Data

Rodríguez Milanés, Cecilia.
Marielitos, balseros and other exiles / Cecilia Rodríguez Milanés.
    p. cm.
ISBN 978-0-9815040-2-5
1. Immigrants--Florida--Fiction. 2. Exiles--Florida--Fiction. 3.
Cubans--Florida--Fiction. I. Title.
PS3618.O359M37 2009
813'.6--dc22
                            2009008212

For my children.
Lili, some of these stories are older than you.
Victor, some of these are younger than you.
All of them are for both of you and all of us.

CONTENTS

A MATTER OF OPINION

CARMEN WAS AWAKENED by the loud sound of a masculine voice in Spanish as the clock radio clicked on. She adjusted the volume in order to begin her morning routine. After making the bed, dressing and brushing her hair and teeth, she headed for the kitchen, the radio's volume still loud enough to hear throughout the apartment. While she was preparing her café con leche, the voice notified her that the upcoming talk show topic would be Marielito prisoners in Atlanta. Carmen's stomach rippled in little knots. Her nephew, Rafael, was an inmate there.

"Won't they leave us in peace," she said out loud to no one. Carmen had been having her coffee alone every morning for five years. Her son, Héctor, had gotten married and left her in 1979, a year before Mariel. Now he lived in Germany, where he was stationed with his army wife. He called once a month though, on the first Sunday, or on the Saturday before if he had a "mission." She glanced at the calendar; he'd be calling this weekend. She took an extra sniff of the ground coffee, covered it, and put the tin back in the refrigerator that was encrusted with bright fruit-shaped magnets.

She thought about her comment and corrected the utterance. "I'm not a Marielita," she mumbled, shaking her head, thinking about Rafael's wild, stringy long hair, his empty gray eyes. "Pobrecito," she touched her cheek, leaving a soapy imprint on her smooth dark skin. The neighbor's children she watched would not be dropped off until 7:30, and she liked to have the place tidy, even if only for an hour, before their toys littered the worn, orange rug. She placed the last of the breakfast dishes in the cupboard with the Formica doors that never closed right.

Carmen remembered, as though it were yesterday, the phone ringing at six in the morning, heralding the inevitable. Like so many others, she was to receive custody of a relative, one of the thousands from what was once termed the Freedom Flotilla, more recently called the Mariel Boatlift.

The young woman at the other end of a seemingly distant phone spoke in broken Spanish, "Do you have relative with the last name Sánchez?"

"Thanks to God," Carmen's face shone with new tears, "Yes." She had given her sister's name to the young man on her block who was taking his speedboat to Mariel to bring back his aunt Chela and uncle Tatín. He had told her that she was the only one he took a name from because she was a "decent woman" who didn't gossip like the others around the neighborhood. The truth was that Carmen didn't gossip because no one talked to her, but she blushed pink through tawny cheeks anyway and quickly wrote down her sister's name and address for the boy. She kissed him, asked God to bless him and provide him with a safe voyage and pushed twenty dollars into his palm.

He would have to make it through the Straits of Florida south from the Keys and into Mariel harbor. She didn't know the voyage directly, but had traced it with her forefinger many times over on a hurricane map printed on the back of a Poe's

Hardware shopping bag. Her husband Luis had attempted that same journey, in the opposite direction, on a half-dozen oil barrels strung together with nets. The seas were unwilling, and pulled him back to Cuba. News of his detention, then torture and finally death at the Boniato prison came via her sister's letters.

After being widowed, Carmen prayed every night that God would allow her younger and only sister, Ester, to come to America. Remembering the wrinkled, stained letters arriving month after month, Carmen longed to have her by her side, just like they had been together as girls, each taking care of the other while mamá y papá worked at their bodega in Luyanó. She and Ester could sew together, embroidering scalloped-edged linens or handkerchiefs, like they did as girls, then they could sell their creations for good money. No one does work like that any more, she muttered, wiping the clear plastic tablecloth of crumbs into her free hand then rubbing them both clean over the garbage. "So much, so much time has passed," she said through the window screen, parting the curtains to facilitate passage of what was left of the morning-cooled breeze into the kitchen. She had tried so many times to comprehend so many events by going over them in her mind, rewinding and reviewing the happenings in her life. This time, like the times before, she found no explanations; the same pictures replayed themselves, unindignant by their rerun status, although of late, they had begun to show signs of wear and tear.

The reel today began with Easter 1980. The Cuban-exile population was ecstatic; everyone with a boat hooked it up to their car and headed for Key West. Companies with large freight-carrying vessels opened their offices at night to accept lists of family members left behind. The radio talk shows were abuzz with news and rumors of what was going on in Mariel. The community leaders and politicians urged calm and patience, but a tidal wave of cars, trucks and vans with boat trailer hitches engulfed the tiny island of Key West. As the first boats arrived, the television cameras incessantly flashed faces across screens in hopes of reuniting families. There were many tear-jerking, heartwarming scenes on the network news programs that inspired Carmen to hope.

The frame flickered to a different time. There she was channeling the grief of early widowhood, then lovingly, painfully rearing her son with an abundant energy that often tired and annoyed the boy. She had not gotten over his move overseas. Shots of aquamarine water flashed; waves and shadows over the Caribbean (these pictures were more faded than the rest). The big stucco steps of the front porch. Ester scooping the jacks in her creamy white palms or brushing Panchita's hair and she brushing Lucila's, her own doll's hair. Flick, flick. Their suitors in the pair of yellow painted wicker chairs waiting in the small patio with Doña Gina from next door, while in their room, they, both solemn and nervous, buttoned each other up for the sixth and last time.

The thought of having her beloved sister with her again made Carmen's head spin so that when the phone rang that early morning she was given life, as we all are, without being asked if we want it.

"Would you receive custody of your nephew?" A tired voice asked.

"Sí, sí, Rafael. Y mi hermana? Ester?" She excitedly pictured her younger sister's caramel skin and green eyes that were identical to her own and their mother's.

"No, señora, eh . . ." The young woman was shuffling through papers as Carmen's mind raced. Gripping the phone in terror, she envisioned her fragile sister and the long sea journey, overcrowded under prepared boats.

"No, señora . . ." There was, it seemed to Carmen, an eternal pause, ". . . solamente su sobrino." The girl went away from the phone as Carmen pondered her nephew who she had not seen since he was a quiet little boy in Miramar twenty years ago.

"Tía?" It was a scratchy, weak voice, not familiar at all, that frightened but moved her. "Is that you?"

"Rafael? Felito, can it really be possible?" She was hesitantly happy, pacing the bedroom as far as the phone cord let her.

"Yes, I am here, but I don't know why, Tía." She assumed he was exhausted and disoriented, so Carmen told him not to worry, that she would come and get him as soon as she could. When she asked about his mother, Rafael told her that "she wasn't any good at these things" and pointed out that "she was always ill, much too weak." In a corner of her mind a lone raft was surrounded by towering waves. Carmen thanked God that her sister was still alive but they were interrupted by the young woman who returned to the phone and told Carmen that Rafael had to be processed. It would take a day or two because of the number of people flooding the temporary immigration center.

By the time Carmen saw him, he was fed and dressed in a large, loud suit, with a clashing tie. He had a check for $200 from the Catholic Services in his pocket. He seemed to be almost smiling, but not quite. Carmen noticed almost immediately that his eyes wandered left and right, then just slid down. Their first embrace was also their last. Rafael was stiff against Carmen's soft, volu-minous bulk; his steel gray eyes gazed flatly past her bright wet, green eyes; his cold cheek collided with her warm, red-painted lips. The more she gushed affection, the more withdrawn he became.

"Felito, mi hijo, qué grande estás!" She started to take his hand but decided only to gesture to him when she saw the thin arms straight at his sides, the shiny nylon shirtsleeves stick-ing out from the polyester topstitched cuff. "How tall you've grown!" He nodded indifferently back to her.

Carmen had used a little of the money she saved from tak-ing care of her landlord's grandchildren in order to hire a taxi. It was her second ride in one. The first, so long ago, had been at her own arrival in Miami in 1961. This trip back to the triplex in Little Havana cost her thirty dollars and fists full of tears. She cried at the happiness of having family again. She cried that Ester wasn't with her and probably would never be. She cried for her nephew's chance for a new life. She cried, but Felito sat rigidly beside her; his eyes avoided her face, periodically, fixing instead on the cars on either side of the street. By the time she opened the door to her apartment, she was stunned into the real-ity that Rafael had no idea why he was in the U.S.A.

"Where will I sleep?" he had said, looking around without emotion.

The radio blared the music that signaled that the morning news was over and that the talk show would commence. The man's deep rolling Spanish echoed from the bedroom.

"Good morning. I am Antonio Guerra, your host for the next hour and the topic of discussion is Mariel prisoners in

Atlanta." The music rose to a crescendo then faded out. Carmen finished folding a towel and put it away with the rest of the linens, then pulled the ironing board out from under her bed. She tried to rush because she didn't want the iron out when the children were around. They might decide to iron their sleeves as she had. Glancing at the thick ragged scar along her bronze arm brought back that afternoon in her mother's kitchen, Ester calmly watching while she scorched her skin. "Children have no sense!" she said out loud, a shudder turning her perspiration cold.

As usual, the rhetoric was full of scathing accusations; Guerra had his artillery ready, soon the words would begin to sting.

"We are all aware of the fact that Castro emptied his prisons and mental asylums when the people resoundingly spoke out by flooding the Peruvian embassy that day in April in 1980. Castro had no choice but to let those brave 10,000 souls leave but he would not and could not permit America and the free world to have propaganda against him and Communism . . ."

Carmen wondered why Guerra was being so delicate. It was unlike him to admit to Castro's ingeniousness. She tested the iron with some spit that instantly sizzled away.

"So when the Cuban community opened its arms and Jimmy Carter opened America's gates, Castro conducted a thorough spring cleaning of all the scum he didn't care to feed, house or tolerate any more . . "

Carmen ironed nervously. Guerra hadn't really gotten going yet; she knew what venom he was capable of. Miami-Cubans loved him for it. His biting insults against Castro, his bombast against Democrats and liberals, his clearly delineated lines between right and wrong, left and right, all this was like a tonic that exiles thrived on. She splashed some starch on her day-robe and yanked off a loose button. Soon, soon he would begin to rail. Carmen braced herself as the steam rose and caressed her face.

"My question to you today is one that our President, Mr. Reagan, and his administration asks us—all of us. Should the United States of America house hardcore criminals, assassins, drug addicts and psychopaths? Those beasts that Castro dumped on our shores in 1980?"

Carmen jerked her fingers away from a still-hot pants' zipper and pushed a pinky into her mouth. Only a blouse and a pillowcase left, she moved quickly, trying unsuccessfully not to listen while her anxiety mounted. She remembered finding some strange seeds in Rafael's shirt pockets.

"Is it necessary, I ask you, that our President must even pose the question? I say the courts are right, correct in their decision to deny them trials. Why should American money and time be spent in convicting self-professed convicts? Send them back. Dump them on Cuban shores in the same fashion that they littered our beaches. No, Castro! We do not want your scum. Have it yourself."

Carmen imagined her husband on the beach at Varadero, surrounded by dogs and rifles. She pulled out the cord, wrapped it around the handle and placed the cooling iron high atop a wire-shelf in the closet. The waters that separated Florida from Cuba are so narrow, yet so powerful, she thought. Carmen, on terra firma, was often shaky. She had had Héctor and his energy to counter the instability of her early years on this new shore. If only . . . Her famous if only. Carmen's full bottom lip quivered while one eye beat the other to a tear. She had gone over it a thousand times. If only he had come with them that terrible morning in 1961, instead of staying back to sell off what was left of their possessions. "I'll be on the next flight," he had said, sending them with what they had saved, $300 sewn into Héctor's dirty diaper. If only he had left the rest. After Carmen had gone there was the missile crisis. After that there were no more flights.

Guerra's voice bristled with excitement. "I see that our telephones are lighting up. Please hold on the line and I'll get to you. Hello, caller number one from Westchester, speak up."

An elderly voice came on the air panting insults at all Marielitos. He said that they had humiliated and degraded the first exiles and their reputation.

The old man ranted while Guerra agreed, crackling in the background with the appropriate disgust. "Marielitos have instilled fear into the Anglo community. Before, Cubans had been respected, part of the whole city; now we're considered foreigners."

Carmen thought of her landlord's daughter who had married a Marielito, now a successful gallery owner on Flagler Street, carrying only pictures by Mariel artists; the fruit market at the corner run by a Marielito, a sweet boy, whom Carmen stopped to chat with whenever she walked by. These viejos, she tisked to herself, what do they know.

Another caller turned out to be a Marielito. Carmen knew Guerra would lure him into his den. "Señor, why is it that you allow your callers to lump all the Mariel exiles together? This last man from Westchester, you didn't even tell him anything."

Sitting with her hands folded on the neat, firm bed, Carmen stared at the glowing green radio numbers from the digital display. Still thirty minutes until the children would arrive. She sighed, smoothing the crocheted bedspread. The caller was weak, she thought; he wouldn't stand a chance against Guerra. Even she could do better than that, she mused, scratching her scalp.

"What have you done for us?" The radio voice sneered. "Tell me, sir, because I assume you are one of those who came through Mariel? Tell me and the public what you have done for us who have sacrificed and worked and slaved for a better life. We who have built this city up and you—you come here and pollute our streets with crime, with murder, rape, burglary, drugs—repugnance! Loathing! That's what I have for you."

Carmen imagined a cheering, applauding chorus behind Guerra at the radio station. She knew that most Miamians agreed with Guerra, labeling sympathizers to the Marielitos' plight also as scum. That last caller didn't stay on the line but half a dozen other callers followed and showered Guerra with approval and support. Carmen picked the lint from the white decorative pillows as she remembered the night the Miami Police had picked Rafael up while he was sleeping in Bicentennial Park a few blocks away. He had taken to staying out all night, worrying Carmen to her wits' end. The call from the police station was reminiscent of that early morning call months before. "Tía, I don't know why I am here." Tears filled her eyes as she reached for an embroidered handkerchief from her dresser drawer, the only recuerdo of Ester's she had brought out of Cuba. Rafael had been in the wrong place at the wrong time, she said to herself. The mayor had decided to clean up the streets of Miami and started downtown, on Biscayne Boulevard, where her nephew had been caught in the dragnet.

"You are 100 percent correct. We should send those bastards back. Give Castro what he deserves . . ."

Carmen glanced at the photographs of her son, husband, sister and nephew on the nightstand. She had no living soul, only these pictures to ease her. There was the army photo of Héctor. Another of him and his dry American wife. There was one photo of Felito as a child. He looked just like his mother when he was little, she smiled to herself. Héctor had been no trouble and Rafael, Ester always said, was a model child. The children Carmen minded were spoiled, rude and hard to control. She couldn't bring herself to love them.

The digits on the clock shifted by. The children would be arriving shortly. She needed to unburden herself. Felito was getting sicker and sicker each day he was in prison. Carmen never told anyone, but she had gone all the way to Georgia to see him. Several times she had even written letters to her congressman over "those helpless creatures of God" jailed without trials. She neared the phone.

Guerra addressed the crimes of the Marielitos. "Gentlemen, ladies, these individuals were in prison in Cuba. They have tattoos to advertise their criminal specialties. We've all heard the stories. Cross-bones for assassins, such and such tattoo for rapists and so on . . . We all are aware of the skyrocketing crime rate in Miami since 1980. How they help the cocaine kingpins with their cheap services as contract killers or dealers. The lazy ones are sleeping in parks, under highways, on the beaches. These individuals are not decent citizens. They do not deserve protection . . ."

Carmen fumbled for the radio station's telephone number in her little book. She did not think, but trembled with anger and sadness instead. The line was busy. She hung up and tried again. Her mouth felt dry. Before the phone finished ringing, someone had picked it up, "QBA, hold on, please." The secretary's Spanish was too crisp, harsh, not from Cuba. Carmen rehearsed in her thoughts. The young sharp voice returned, "You must turn down your radio so that you can talk. Where are you calling from?"

"From Hialeah," she lied, stuttering at first. Carmen decided not to hide her voice. She didn't like to call during Guerra's show, but today . . .

"You are caller ten. Please listen for when Mr. Guerra asks you to speak."

"Yes, I will," Carmen began but the hold button cut her off. She reached over and turned the radio down very low. The callers were frenzied sharks snapping at Guerra's bloodied chum.

"We first generation Cubans resent the Marielitos coming to Miami and ruining our reputation. I, myself, am considering following the many thousand Anglo-Americans who have moved out of Dade County into Broward."

Guerra was letting the callers express themselves. Perhaps Carmen would be able to make her point. "You're next, señora. Stand by and be ready," the voice said, before disappearing again. Carmen used the choking hurt to buffer herself for the onslaught.

"Caller ten from Hialeah, speak up."

"Mr. Guerra, you and a great number of your audience believe that no one of any value escaped Castro's communism in 1980."

"Oh, señora, you are wrong." He paused. "There are a few."

CECILIA RODRÍGUEZ MILANÉS

"Mr. Guerra, you are too smug. Your family is free here, wealthy here." He was biding his time, letting her have her say. "What of those families, those persons whose entire families are still in Cuba waiting?" Carmen spoke rapidly for she knew her courage or airtime would not last long. "What of those put in prison without trials in Cuba and now imprisoned here in America, the land of the free? They were never allowed to stand before their accusers to defend themselves. What comfort do you give those men's wives, their children, mothers and sisters?"

"Señora, those individuals were in prison before they came to this country. They were permitted to come to America so that they could create havoc, that's all. Castro was not being a humanitarian when he unleashed those animals—criminals, addicts and lunatics—onto our streets." Guerra took a breath that dared Carmen to interrupt him.

"I take it you trust Castro's judgments?" She said at last, quietly, pausing then knowing that the click and tone meant that her words would fly across the airwaves, over the troubled seas and hungry sharks. She got up to open the door for the landlord's children now shouting through the kitchen screen while the radio whispered back, " . . . you trust Castro's judgments?"

LA BUENA VIDA

THE WAITERS HUDDLED between servings to exchange Marielito jokes, and since Alvarez's was the best, they made him tell it again. "A Cuban gasoline station owner is advising his employees, `Listen to me; don't be stupid. I tell you this for your own good. If a white man comes to rob the station, forget about the gun; leave it in the cash drawer. Just give him the money. It's not worth it. Likewise, if a black man comes to steal, you give him the money—curse his mother when he leaves—but really it is not worth the trouble. You may lose your life. But, listen to me now, if one of those god damned Marielitos comes here to rob this station, you blow the son-of-a-bitch's brains out, you understand?'"

Alvarez laughed with the other waiters until he noticed the manager motioning for him to come over to the kitchen. Next to Mr. Rosenfield was a thin young man with pockmarks in the hollows of his cheeks.

"Alvarez, this is Juan, the new dishwasher. He doesn't speak English. Show him the job and give `em the low down. I don't want any trouble with this one." The manager walked swiftly away.

Alvarez handed Juan a food-smeared smock and cap, then

directed him towards a double stainless steel sink. Nearby a steaming industrial dishwasher droned. Juan smiled at the thought of his luck—la suerte del cubano—at having gotten a job in Miami just like the one he used to have in Cuba.

"Why do I always have to deal with you people?" Alvarez spoke in a mumbled Spanish as he led Juan around the illuminated kitchen. Juan noticed that Alvarez's head jerked a lot when he spoke to him, like many Miami-Cubans did. He had decided that these motions were part of the changed Spanish that his new old compatriots spoke.

"This is where you are to work. The glasses will be brought to you." Alvarez cut off many of the words' endings in his speedy Spanish—he must be from la habana—and Juan's face contorted in an effort to keep up with him. A tall black man, also with a dirty smock and hat, crashed an overflowing tray into a nearby sink, startling Juan. The black man looked Juan over, and Alvarez said, "This is the way the dishes are turned over to you."

"Gracias, señor," Juan called out but Alvarez had already pushed through the heavy swinging doors, past the short corridor, into the plush carpeted and draped dining room. A glimpse at Alvarez's embroidered red and purple velvet jacket before the cool darkness past the second set of doors enveloped him stirred Juan. Ah, to wear that jacket, feel that coolness, the young man sighed to himself, "Algún día . . ."

From where Juan stood he could see the doors flick back and forth all day. Sometimes they looked animated to him, defending the heavy curtains and starchy linens, permitting only the velvet-jacketed men inside. Opening the faucet, he would let hot water run over the lipstick-smeared wine glasses. Within a month, Juan had been promoted to the crystal stemware. He treasured these, making them squeaky clean, watching the rainbows in the suds and imagining the painted lips that had been pressed to them. On slow afternoons, he often meandered by the dining room doors in that middle chamber between the brightly lit, richly aromatic kitchen, and the dark, flower-perfumed salon where strange whispering voices buzzed.

"I told you to stay away from the dining room," the maitre'd chastised in vain. Once he realized that Juan understood little or nothing of what he said, he attempted to communicate with his hands while he spoke more slowly. It was painful to Juan how the man's mouth opened wide. "I. Said. Away. From. Here. No. More. Standing. Here." Then he spoke to anyone who cared to listen and understood, "It's not enough that you people come here and everything is given to you, but no, you go on welfare, you take and take and still you want more." His tilted head shook violently from side to side.

"Si, señor," Juan nodded, then questioned one of the Haitian men about what the man had said, but the Haitian responded in a strangely familiar tongue something about Juan's hair sticking up and that he must keep it under the cap. Juan felt his limp, oiled hair beneath his hat and surmised that it must have had something to do with the poor man's aching head.

On another slow afternoon Juan peered through the door's small windows into the dining room and saw a large woman whose stiff, platinum hair was pulled away from her puffy face to accentuate two huge emerald earrings. A matching necklace was almost lost in a hilly bosom, which rose when she inhaled. The maitre'd caught Juan gaping from across the room and expertly maneuvered between the customers and desert carts without so much as fluttering a tablecloth. His furrowed brow was clearer to Juan than his sharp jabbing tongue. Juan answered the barking sounds with "Si, señor" while the man pointed him back to the sudsy sinks.

Juan recalled the kitchen manager's instructions, "Glasses, that's all; just glasses." The boss didn't like the way the machines left the "crystals"—cordials, sherry, brandy, fine glasses of all kinds, shapes he had never seen before. Juan liked to look at how the stark light would shine on the cut edges of the goblets as he polished them. He would hold them up and examine each one just as he had seen the people do on his second cousin Mario's large color television set.

Mario didn't think his job was important but Juan insisted that $110 for working five ten-hour days was like a gift from God. After all, he had argued, in Cuba he had hand washed hundreds of plates, six days a week, for 45 pesos a month, with no cool curtained dining room to look into. The waiters back there wore thin cotton guayaberas. Now he was getting paid every week and had Sundays off. Surely this was the good life, la buena vida. Mario always agreed with him that compared to Cuba, Miami was paradise. Juan smiled to himself, they got along well. Whenever his cousin's wife, Lupe, talked about the Marielito escoria, Mario always defended him and reminded her of Juan's job, the fact that he contributed money for the rent and his quiet manners. Lupe now made it a point to criticize Marielitos whenever Juan was home and Mario was not.

Juan carefully measured the extra soap he needed; he was proud he didn't squander like the others. He began to hum a tune he had picked up from the transistor radio Mario gave him and shifted his feet below the long grimy smock. He stopped swaying his hips at the thought that he should keep his radio tuned to the North American stations. That was his cousin's advice. Already in the months at his job he had developed quite a vocabulary: sherry, wine, champagne, highball, spotty, streaks, chipped, detergent . . . He marveled at how many words were similar to their Spanish equivalents: champaña, highball, detergente. From now on, Juan said to himself, he would really make an effort to learn English, but it was so hard when almost everyone he knew spoke only his language.

On the way up his street, Juan noticed Mario's pickup truck in front of the house and wondered why he was home so early—he usually worked until 6:00, but it was only 4:00. Many other cars that didn't belong to the family were parked on the grass in front of the house and next door, in Martica's driveway. Juan wondered why they would have a party in the middle of the week before Mario was supposed to be home, but then again, in this country, you did not need a reason to have a party.

He rushed to the doorbell and tripped on the step, slamming his knee against the jalousie glass panes in the door. His cousin's ten-year-old son burst outside. Pepito's face was red and swollen and he had on fresh clothes. His hair was wet and in place. Juan took the young boy's puffed cheeks into his still wrinkled fingertips and quietly asked what was wrong.

"My daddy died, Juan." Both of their faces grimaced at the words.

Juan bent down to embrace the boy, but Pepito turned away crying for his mother. She came to the doorway, scowled at Juan and threw her hands in her face as she cursed.

"My cousin," Juan spoke softly into the hands, trying to

make the words pull the tight red fingers apart.

"Prima, I'm so sorry. I feel it very much."

Later they all went to one of the many Cuban funeral parlors in Miami. The widow Lupe, her parents Sonia and Eduardo, the boys Pepito and Carlos, various aunts and uncles, and herds of cousins sat at the wake all night. The next morning the directors closed the chapel for a couple of hours so that the immediate family could go home and freshen up for the services that afternoon. They had the run of the place since the other three chapels were vacant, and it seemed to give Lupe great satisfaction to know that with every delivery of flowers more of the cold paneled walls in the capilla where Mario lay would be obscured and perfumed by tall elaborate wreaths.

Juan was amazed at the number of people who came through the chapel. Face after face expressed sympathy, gossiped, told jokes, smoked, drank espresso or dozed on the maroon overstuffed vinyl couches and easy chairs throughout the parlor rooms. So many of them came through the stained glass doors and Juan still did not know all of their names, yet none made any effort to express their pésames to him or hardly even acknowledge him. It had always angered Mario that they were so rude to Juan, but now no one was there to point out their incivility.

The day of the funeral Juan put on his only good long-sleeve shirt; it had all its buttons and no pulls. He wore a pair of brown polyester pants and black patent leather Capezios that Carlos had tired of. Juan wanted to show his respect by wearing a jacket but the boys were 14 and 10 and neither could accommodate Juan's slight but long-armed build. He did not want to ask Lupe for one of Mario's, but before they all left the crowded house her father handed him a heavy plaid coat and wide tie.

"Gracias, don Eduardo. I did not want to bother you," Juan said, but the older man had not spoken to Juan since he arrived in Miami and didn't seem to want to break his silence just yet.

They did not all fit into the black limousine so Juan asked one of Lupe's cousins from Westchester for a ride. The day was as bright and hot as any other August day in Miami and Juan hoped a rain cloud would pass over that would cool them off for a while. Since there had been a short service at the capilla the night before, the rest of the rituals were performed at the grave. The funeral dragged on as the priest spoke in a refined Spanish, but Juan couldn't concentrate because of a noisy backhoe a few yards away pushing a mound of sandy soil into a deep rectangle. A pair of cemetery workers leaning on shovels watched the funeral and waited. Moving off, Juan decided to say a prayer over his aunt Zoila's grave a few yards away. When he had first come to Miami, Mario had shown him where she was buried. They had talked there, over Mario's grandmother's and Juan's great aunt's tomb, about the sacrifices she had made for Mario by sending him out of Cuba when he was fourteen to evade the mandatory military training for youths. Mario had recounted tales of the time he and dozens of other young Cuban boys were under the care of Father Walsh, that "great humanitarian" as Mario would say.

Juan thought about Mario, Zoila and then his own mother back in Cuba. She had encouraged him to come to the United States the day the underground radio transmitted the first reports of the storming of the gates at the Peruvian Embassy. As always, she was right when she said "Your cousin Mario will help you. He is a good man." Again and again she had persisted, "Here there is nothing. Over there, you will never want for anything." Juan knew his mother would not be mistreated if he left since she was already retired from the workforce. Also, his sister's husband was a member of the Party and could prevent the government from penalizing her through reduced rations. He had turned the thoughts over and over in his mind the next few days at his job in the Hotel Riviera. He even considered jumping over the concrete wall onto the embassy grounds but soldiers with rifles had pulled up in trucks within twenty-four hours of the first gatecrashers. After the Cuban guards were stationed, leaving seemed an impossibility, but his mother continued to pray and seek counsel from the santero who lived next door.

His mind came to the scenes at the port of Mariel, the sleek racing boat with the angry young man who did not want to take Juan aboard, but who gave in when the guards said they would take the man's grandmother back, the processing tents in Key West, the air-conditioned bus ride to Miami, his cousin's smiling face, and thousands of other smiling faces that soon faded. These thoughts troubled and held him so that the caravan of cars with the hearse leading had long pulled away from the cemetery gates and left him very much alone among the tombstones. He started to run but then turned back. The gravesite was deserted but for the mountain of gladiolus, carnations, chrysanthemums and tuber roses.

The rain cloud Juan had wished for came around and drenched him as he walked south on Calle Ocho. He was only a couple of miles away from his cousin's house though it could have been two hundred miles since Juan had no idea where he was. He only knew that the tall buildings of downtown Miami were towards the bay, east of his street and that cielito lindo, the roof of the county jail, was always to his left when he took the bus back from work.

The torrential rain beat his hunched back and booming thunderbolts charged the air, until, just as suddenly as it had arrived, the cloud moved off to the west. Twenty minutes later, it was bright and hot again; only now, the streets were wet and the air seemed cleaner, heavily accentuated with a lushness of replenished foliage. Juan had turned the old man's coat inside out to spare it but the tie had fallen into a puddle and was soaked through.

By the time the sun's last rays completely left the indigo and orange streaked sky, Juan had circled Little Havana three times looking for a specific stately Royal palm and a certain trio of old men who always sat around on folding chairs at the particular corner he was searching for. "It's useless," Juan said to himself as he stretched his legs out before the bus bench. A smelly, long-haired sleeping man had already claimed three fourths of the bench and now he turned over, coughed noisily, and kicked him.

"Eh, qué pasa?" Juan questioned the snoring man. He shifted his hips over away from him. Soon a nearly empty bus pulled up and Juan noticed it had the same sign as the one he took from Miami Beach and stepped on. He took the customary three heavy silver coins and dropped them into the clicking glass box. Within minutes of boarding he saw his palm tree and buzzed the driver to let him off.

The relatives' cars were gone, but all of the lights in the house were on. Lupe opened the door before Juan could reach for the knob. The standing fan in the corner of the Florida room shifted hot air from side to side. Sonia, Lupe's mother, announced that she was going to check in on her husband as Juan crossed the threshold. His greeting to them all was cut off by Lupe's words.

"Don't tell me anything. What the hell do you think this is? A hotel? My nerves will not handle all of this." Her agitated voice seemed aimed at his already sunken heart. She would not let him interrupt her, no one else ever could either, but he knew that Lupe had to let off steam just as she often did at the boys or Mario. He noticed that his person was a subject curiously absent from her harangue.

"I cannot go on like this. I will not take any more. Do you know what it is that this man should die now? Now that we have Carlos starting San Bernardo's at $3,000 a year? Ay, Dios mío! And for what? To keep him away from trouble and now he has no father."

Uncontrollably tapping his feet on the polished terrazzo floor, Carlos rolled his eyes away from his mother and her intermittent sobs. Pepito was still bleary-eyed but his hair was now tangled and he had long abandoned his navy blazer for Hawaiian-printed shorts and a matching shirt. The younger boy's eyes lingered over the face of the dark television screen as the older one earnestly bit his cuticles. No one said anything to Juan as he hurried past. He rushed to hang up don Eduardo's jacket, deciding it was better to lie about the man's tie and say he had lost it on the bus.

Now Lupe was going on weepily about Mario's virtues, something that took them all by surprise.

"He worked until he dropped. Imagine that, the poor man has a heart attack right at the job site, mercy on us, Santísima

María. He worked and slaved and even gave up his vacations. You boys were too young to remember when he worked days and nights. I used to be at home with both of you. Mario only slept and ate here. His life was a serfdom and for what, now he's buried. Ah, it always happens like that. God help me now."

Poor woman, he thought, her compañero gone and now with two boys to rear. It won't be easy for her but at least she has her family. Juan decided to help in whatever way he could. Maybe she would like him better now. Lupe talked quickly and loudly while Juan thought about their situation and imagined profiles and animals in the swirled colors of the large floor tiles.

She tired herself out by one in the morning. The boys were already in bed but Juan did not want to be rude and walk away from the grieving and distracted woman. Finally, she put her head down on the glass-top iron wrought table and fell asleep. Juan nodded off on the sofa without pulling out his bed in order to avoid waking her with the noise and motion. In the morning Lupe's eyes were clear, her pointed fist firm when she nudged him awake.

"Listen. Pay attention because I'm only going to tell you once. This is the last time I will permit you in my house. You are no relative of mine. When you leave today, don't come back. Go and find yourself another place to live. There will be no room for you here ever again, understand?"

Although still disoriented, Juan immediately understood Lupe's tone; it was the same one she used to give Mario ultimatums. He looked around and noticed by the clock that he was late for work. The boys were gone and don Eduardo was there standing near his daughter with a wooden mop in his hands. He could hear doña Sonia washing clothes in the rear of the house;

she always cleared the room when Lupe took that tone. "Your things are in a bag outside. Don't make me call the police. I'm sure they would love to throw another Marielito in jail."

Her father approached him with the palo. He raised it as Juan tried to collect his thoughts in order to answer. Lupe stepped back toward the kitchen as the frowning man moved closer to him.

"Lárgate de aquí, hijo de puta," were the first and last words Juan heard from Eduardo as he rushed to the screen door. Outside he found a plastic grocery bag in the grass. The metal frame slammed shut followed by the clinking close of the jalousie windowpanes and Lupe's curses. Overturning the bag's contents, Juan found two undershirts, one green and white short-sleeve terrycloth pullover that he changed into as he walked towards the bus stop, a pair of jeans cuffed at the hems, three jockey shorts, a razor and his bright red radio. He looked up a moment at the mustard-colored house with red barrel tiles. There were rooms in that small house that he had never even seen—Sonia and Eduardo's, Mario and Lupe's. He shook his head low to his flat chest. Mario's mis-parked truck cast a shadow over grass, which needed cutting; weeds were shooting up through some cracks in the concrete driveway. Pobre mujer, he sighed as he repacked his belongings. Juan hastened to the corner where he shuffled his feet awaiting the next Lincoln Road bus to Miami Beach. At present all he could focus on were the passing cars, most of them new, that is, less than his thirty years. In Cuba, the only "new" cars belonged to the ambassadors and these were drab Russian or Czech models, so unlike these shiny colorful autos which streamed through Miami.

Alvarez took great pleasure in firing the newest Marielito. He poured forth all of his energy into the dismissal and the waiters stood close by to relish every word of it. The confused Juan did not take pleasure in the hyperbole and similes that Alvarez let rip into his face for the young downcast man was preoccupied with the realization that now he would never be able to wear the purple velvet jacket or go into the cool darkness of the dining room. His disappointment was so great that he was not aware that the dismissal speech was over and Alvarez had to push him out the kitchen's backdoor.

Juan wandered the neighborhood and then across the Arthur Godfrey Causeway a couple of times before making his way back to the bus stop to return to la sagüecera, as latinos referred to that Southwestern quarter of Miami. With the sun burning his now red cheeks, he stood at the corner and remembered the day when two military guards had come for him at the Hotel Riviera and asked if he had any family in Usa. Before he could reply, they told him if he wanted to leave that he could—all this in front of the others. Right there, before their narrowed and cutting eyes, he said he would. Stones, branch limbs and spit flew toward Juan when they "escorted" him back to the apartment to gather only what could be carried, which could not include money, jewelry, passport, birth certificate, or any document. And, of course, he would be allowed to take leave of his mother who just cried silently; the only words she could utter were "mi hijo."

At the corner of Forty-first Street and Prairie Avenue, old dark-suited Jewish men shuffled past Juan, reminded, perhaps by his contorted face, of themselves. Juan was oblivious to the Yiddish, English, and even Spanish spoken all around him on that corner; he was full of the beatings he had received from the young guards once in their custody, the dog attacks while waiting for a boat at the Port of Mariel and the rough sea voyage through the Gulfstream. He wiped the perspiration from his forehead with his sleeve and stepped off the curb to check on the sign of the approaching bus. Once aboard he fell again into deep distraction with images of Mario, rifle butts, his mother's eyes, velvet jackets, swaying palms, painted lips and Lupe's angry words, so that tears he had saved for so long finally flooded his eyes and spilled onto the plastic bag on his lap. Me votáron, he said to himself and then to the two small white-haired women sitting across from him, "They threw me out." The women ignored him and continued their running commentary on how truly terrible a place Miami had become. Attempting a kind of composure at last, Juan quickly wiped his face with a pair of underwear from the bag and cleared his knotted throat. He moved through the aisle and stepped into those streets, mean with Marielitos and all sorts of rejects, those whose families refused to continue to sponsor or support them. Those who could find neither comfort nor commerce from the first waves of exiles from that island so fondly remembered as La Perla de las Antillas.

With several hours of daylight still remaining, Juan decided he would ask for a job in any of the dozens of Cuban restaurants that lined Calle Ocho. He knew that the five dollars pinned in his underwear would not buy him a place to stay for the night, but if he found a job today he would at least know what vicinity to sleep in. Buoyed up by hopes of work, along with his three-month experience and growing English, Juan felt strangely confident he would soon find a job. He stopped at a window in a market for a cafecito and asked the red-lipped and rouge-cheeked woman whose orange hair stuck to her neck if they needed help.

"I wash dishes, glasses, mop the floors, anything." Juan spoke slowly, gently.

She handed him a paper cup filled with water along with a shot of espresso. "We use very little plates. Maybe you should go to a bigger restaurant." She smiled at him, exposing yellowed, uneven teeth. The smile and her eyes told him she was one like himself—a Marielita. Most of the other exiles were so different in their ways and even looks.

Juan walked up and down the street looking for empleo until his feet ached. He was grateful that the day had turned overcast, so he sat in Domino Park to watch the cars pass and tried to read the ads on the sides of the buses while the thick black-and-white tiles were slapped down on tables behind and around him. Most of the bus ads were in Spanish so he didn't get much practice reading. Once rested, he got up and crossed the street to La Esquina de Tejas—the name of a famous restaurant he used to go to in Havana with his father when he was alive. He wondered if the owner was the same as he went around the side to the back and scratched on the grimy screen door of the kitchen. He called to a balding stocky man who asked Juan what he wanted.

"Yes, please, I'd like to speak to the manager, sir."

"He's not here. You know him?" The man wiped his greasy hands on wide hips.

"No, señor. I need work. I wash dishes, glasses, anything. I take any . . ."

The man cut him off, "No hay trabajo," and kicked the inner door closed with his dirty white shoe. Juan tried the other four restaurants on that block, all with the same refrain, "no work."

At a busy intersection where three buses waited for the light to change, Juan thought about boarding again, but he had no place to go. He was also afraid of ending up in Overtown which had too recently been burning in riots. He had never fully learned the cause of the flames dotting Miami's black neighborhoods; it puzzled him to see the high columns of smoke choking the red sun many afternoons in a row. Mario had said it was because the police had killed a black man and Juan usually took his word, but somewhere in his mind it didn't seem to be enough of a reason. He wondered who the man was and why the Latin radio stations warned listeners to stay within their own parts of the city. Juan felt comfortable with his Haitian friends Jean-Pierre and Henri from the restaurant, but his experience with North American blacks was limited to Johnnie, another man he worked with, who led him to believe that hating Cubans was not uncommon among North American blacks; he could not confirm this however.

Juan couldn't count on finding Jean-Pierre or Henri if he got lost getting off from a bus in Liberty City, so he continued walking toward Flagler until there weren't any more big restaurants, only bookstores, record shops and botánicas, where life-size saint statues crowded up the windows. Peering into the packed storefronts, the figures looked alive to Juan; crowned martyrs were covered with beads and dust, surrounded by flowers. For a time in Havana, the botánicas were counter-revolutionary and could only be found in obscure neighborhoods, never advertised and always watched by members of The Party. His mother would have loved to see these, he thought, for she was a "daughter" of Yemayá, the beautiful blue-robed saint of the oceans.

He reached a brightly lit supermarket and decided to get something to eat since it was already dark and many of the shops were closing or closed. The air conditioning chilled him as he stepped through the automatic doors. He hurried past, afraid of being struck by them as they swung so close to his shoulders.

A pint of milk, saltines and Vienna salchichas set him back two dollars but he was content with his meal and had three full bags of crackers left over for tomorrow's breakfast. The cold milk coated his throat and would ease his now rumbling stomach as he came to a clearing by an underpass to the expressway ramp. This Juan recognized as the entrance Mario always took to go to Lupe's cousin's house in Hialeah. The concrete sloped all around him and a weedy, trash-strewn hill met the angle of the road. The land was partially fenced off and Juan saw a torn cardboard refrigerator box pushed up against the section of chain link that was under the highway. Canvas sacks and newspapers were matted to the ground nearby and Juan noticed a bundle of rags and assorted shoes next to an immense concrete column.

"You there!" A voice boomed from behind. Juan turned to face a shirtless old man waving a baseball bat at him.

"Get away from here. I ain't got no money. Leave me alone. Go away now, you hear!" The man approached, smelling of sardines and sweat. Juan pushed his palms out, dropping his plastic bag. The man jerked it away menacingly, holding the bat while he tore the plastic apart. Juan painfully watched the man throw his clothes and food all over the ground; he stopped only when he found the radio. He smiled as he turned it on.

"Eh, please sir, my radio. No tuyo, my . . . give back, please," Juan struggled to make him understand but the man wasn't paying attention to him.

"You listen to country?" The man had dropped the bat and was synchronizing a particular station.

"Con-tree?"

"Yea, you know. Only two kinds of music; country and western," the old man chuckled then started humming in tune to a melody on the air.

"Ah, country, jes, jes," Juan proudly answered the way his cousin had taught him, "Now, my country es United Estates."

"No, you idiot. Country music. Johnny Cash. Willie Nelson." He sang a few lyrics.

Juan wondered what nationality and money had to do with his radio and music. "I sorry. My English . . . little." He gestured with his thumb and forefinger to show how little.

"You one a them Murielitos, ain't cha?" Squinting a cloudy eye, the man surveyed Juan and drew the bat close again.

"Please, sir. My radio, please." Juan held out his trembling hand. The old man paused, squinted his other eye, then handed it over. Relieved, Juan graciously thanked him and reached out to shake his hand but the man, thinking the worst, had automatically raised the bat to his shoulder again. Juan cringed, then used his hands and pleading eyes to make him understand, which worked considerably better than his English.

"Well, all right then." The man put the bat down and crossed his spotted hands over a caved-in chest. "You look harmless."

"Please, sir," Juan began, "My name es Juan Piñero González." He held out a shaking hand once more.

"Shoot, all them bandits offa those banana boats 'round here would just a soon slit yer throat then shake yer hand." As the man laughed to himself, the nervousness began to slip away from Juan's anxious face.

"Thank you bery much, sir." Juan took the man's thick hand and covered it with his soft fingers.

"Well, how you do Juan Fernandez?" The old man laughed again and shook his hand back. "My name's Bill Kingston."

"González. Juan Piñero González," he corrected, "Mister King-ston." He continued to smile at the gray haired man who now knew his name and no longer waved a bat at him.

"Bill, call me Bill." He motioned for Juan to sit down on a cinder block while he went around the pillar for another. Juan sat down this time without worrying about where he would spend the night.

Juan shared what was left of his dinner while Bill offered his wine. They ate and drank without exchanging words and then fell asleep leaning against the column while, from time to time, cars zoomed overhead. In the morning Juan's eyes snapped open to the brilliant rising sun. Bill was not around and for a few moments he could not remember where he was and began to moan. Bill returned to his hunched companion.

"Whadsa matter, buddy, got a hangover?" He touched Juan on the shoulders, startling him into a wide smile.

"Oh, you awright. Had some bidness to tend to but I got us some breakfast." His outstretched palms cradled a long loaf of hot Cuban bread.

"Ah, qué bueno!" Juan's stomach growled. "Bery good."

Bill, tore the steaming bread, gave Juan half and squatted down. Juan kneeled next to him. They greedily took big bites of the soft, doughy loaf.

"Gracias, eh, thank you, Bill," Juan said between mouthfuls.

"Son, you need to learn you some more English." Bill tore the bread bag open, pulled a green crayon from his ripped pant pocket and scraped the tip on the concrete column before taking it on the white wrinkled paper. He wrote "English" in an artful even hand.

"I speak little English," Juan answered with his fingers pinched together. He recited the words he could recall from the restaurant: water, goblet, soap, eh, crystal, wine glass, water, eh, sink, apron, dirty, spotty, eh . . ." until Bill interrupted him.

"Good, good, but you need to learn more, more English." He pointed to the word then wrote the "job" on the paper and showed it to Juan. "You need more English to get a job. You too young to be bumming around like ole Bill here. Hem, let's see. Work—what's that word you people say, eh, tra-ba-jo? Yea, that's it. Shit, I'm a god damned bilingual! To work—is to have a trabajo, see; a job." He pointed to the word.

Pleased as he was to understand something of what Bill said, Juan tried to talk.

"Sí, sí; trabajo. My 'job'—wash dishes, glasses," Juan shook his head, adding, "no more; finished."

"No problem. You'll get another job," Bill smiled into Juan's sad eyes. "With more English, you will get another job, okay?"

A hot thrill flushed through Juan's veins and into his sunken cheeks; he nodded exaggeratedly and took Bill's hands to shake them. "Yes, sir, thank you, sir."

"Bill, amigo, Bill." He grinned, putting a bony arm covered with sagging skin around Juan's slight shoulders.

For the next few weeks, the men moved the cardboard abode from underpass to underpass, went to the public showers on the boardwalk in Miami Beach, ate at the Catholic hospice whenever they longed for a hot meal, picked up over-ripe mangoes from the Little Havana neighborhood to their hearts' content and took turns after dark watching out for the "other" street people who wandered the night. The vigorous campaign to teach Juan English met with great results once Bill decided he wasn't going to say anything else in his piss-poor Spanish.

Bill got a McDonald's application and taught Juan how to fill it out perfectly. Once Juan knew how without any assistance, they walked to the nearest restaurant downtown. Juan took the pen Bill had found and carefully put all the correct answers in the appropriate spaces. He turned the application in while Bill paced the parking lot. The Cuban manager, Mr. Gómez, looked Juan over in disgust and remarked out loud that since they were hard pressed for night crew, he could start work the next evening from 6:00 p.m. till closing at $3.35 an hour. Then he handed Juan a blue-and-white striped, polyester uniform. Juan hurried to the men's room and tossed his clothes over the stall and zippered the tunic up. The pants loosely danced on his thighs. He knew he would gain weight as soon as he started eating regularly. With his clothes tucked under his arm, he rushed out to show the manager; Bill saw him from the window facing the parking lot and flashed a smile.

"Fine, fine. I'll see you tomorrow. Come in around five for some training." Gómez jammed his lips shut, indicating that that was all.

Juan turned around and walked away humming the jingle Bill had taught him, "You deserve a break today . . ." The older man slapped his knee and laughed out once the beaming new employee was outside.

That night, they celebrated with some Budweiser and pretzels while listening to a baseball game on Juan's radio. Someone came during the night while they were both asleep and took most of Bill's shoes, leaving behind only a pair of high-topped sneakers with very little of their soles left. Bill was pained and irritated by the theft, which deflated most of Juan's joy. Juan bitterly blamed himself for not staying alert and promised he would buy Bill more shoes with his first paycheck.

Pacified and hungry, they walked to a nearby fruit and veg-etable market and bought some finger bananas, apples and sug-arcane stalks. The afternoon breezed by while they watched all the young college students boisterously returning through the streets from a victorious football game at the Orange Bowl. Fraternity banners and orange and green pom-poms overflowed the car windows, and Bill and Juan yelled back at the incoherent cheers. When the church bells gonged four times, a wide smile fixed on Juan's face as he turned to Bill and said, "I am going to work."

While he dressed carefully, Bill gave him some last minute advice. "Always go to work early. You want to make a good impression." Juan agreed as he straightened the blue and white cap over his slicked-back hair.

"Smile, too. Always smile all the time; it drives `em crazy."

"Bill, you come downtown with me?" Juan gestured as he tied his shoelaces against the fence.

"Naw, buddy." Bill patted him on the back and gave him a peppermint swirl candy. "Go ahead, you don't need me any-more."

"Oh. Oh, Okay, Bill." Biting his pale lower lip, Juan tilted his head a bit and pressed both hands across his chest. "I feel bery much for you . . . what you do for me. I never forget it, Bill."

The old man pushed his lids closed to hold back the flooding warmth in his eyes. "Aw, come on." His voice cracked slightly then regained its depth. "You're gonna be late for work. Go on now, git."

They moved in different directions, but both carried away similar sentiments. Juan walked purposely, one foot firmly in front of the other. His route led him through a construction area beneath the new, elevated train. Gingerly he stepped over and around whatever could soil his uniform, lingering beneath the cool darkness. Smiling, grateful, thinking of Bill and his new job, he was a happy man.

Within that very hour, Juan was stabbed, for no reason, by another boatlift exile. But that did not disturb Juan's heart. In fact, while the blood oozed through his striped polyester tunic and onto the sidewalk, he was imagining his friend under the highway waiting for him with a red and purple jacket.

LA PAREJA

"I'M HERE," SALVADOR called out through the crack in between the door and the chain. He could hear Gabi rushing up from the big chair in front of the television to let him in.

"How goes it?" Gabi asked. There was a light kiss after closing the door; then they walked one after the other through the narrow hall toward the little kitchen.

"Look at what I brought," Salvador said. In his hands he held up a bunch of dark purple grapes. "Aren't these beautiful?"

"Where'd you get 'em?" Gabi plucked one off and popped it through narrow lips. "Qué rico!"

"Good, eh?" Salvador smiled, nodding his head. "A street vendor. Near the airport. I was stopped at the light and they looked too good to pass up." Gabi took the bunch from his hands and began to rinse them in the sink. Salvador went around for his stool. They never got around to getting a real dinette set so their meals were taken at the wide counter between the large opening separating the kitchen from the dining/living room. It was cool and very bright in the apartment even when the sheer yellow curtains were all drawn. The curtains had been left folded on top of the dumpster in the parking lot one morning and Gabi had rescued, washed and mended them.

"Ay, what a day at that store." Salvador sighed, waiting for Gabi to sit at the stool across from him on the kitchen side of the counter. "Who the hell ever told me to work for Cuban Jews!" He watched Gabi's narrow shoulders square.

"Don't be that way, Dodo. That's a good job. At least you can get a discount on clothes." Gabi's thick brows furrowed over large-lidded eyes; his shoulders returned to their habitual slump as his voice rose. "You make a dollar more an hour than me and I don't even get time for lunch!"

His lower lip was slightly quivering. Salvador reached over to touch his arm. "Qué pasa, mi vida?" His soft hazel eyes met Gabi's moist brown ones.

Salvador got up, took a dirty cup away, sat back down and still, Gabi was shaking. He couldn't understand what the big fuss was all of sudden. Gabi had been working in that store since they moved back to Miami, about three years ago. Once in a while he complained about the place, but never like this.

Salvador banged his bare heels against the legs of the stool, thinking, then stopped his legs and got up to bring Gabi a roll of tissue. He returned to his seat at the counter and looked away from Gabi's sniffling, out the window. Their second-floor apartment was in the rear of the building, facing the parking garage of the larger building next door. Salvador watched some kids riding their bikes down the ramp and skidding to a halt at the bottom. He turned his eyes back to Gabi when he spoke up again.

"I don't know how much more I can take from him, Dodo." Gabi lifted his densely bearded chin and gently shook it from side to side, fighting back a squeaking voice. "Today, I was very close to sending that man to hell."

"Gabi," Salvador spoke slowly, "please tell me. What happened?"

Their eyes met again in a pause. The air conditioner's motor adjusted itself, cranking up loudly, all but drowning out the screeching of the bicycle tires outside. Gabi ran a thin hand with long fingers through his wavy hair. "You know what that animal did today? I was seeing to some Colombians who were going to buy some watches. They wanted only Japanese ones, automatics, men's and women's. I had been waiting on them for about three quarters of an hour when Oscar returned from the other store. Incidentally, he left me alone from 9:15 to 11:30 and, of course, I didn't even have the key to close the doors in case I had to go to the bathroom or anything . . ."

"Ay, but that's typical of that brute, Gabi." Salvador had not meant to be sarcastic. He tried again. "You have to demand that he leave you the key when he goes away like that." That was better, he said to himself, pulling the wrinkled shirt out from his well-fitted pants.

"Anyway, that's not why I'm pissed." Gabi raised his hand as if stopping traffic. "I had given these people good prices because they were going to buy about a dozen and I could tell they would come back because I've seen them around Lincoln Road before. One of them is very stocky. An enormous belly. I swear, he looks like he's about to give birth. I remembered him because when Luisito was still working, we saw him one day in front of the store rubbing his stomach. Well, you know Luisito, he made some cutting remark about him that I can't remember now, even if you killed me. So, here I am with these people and there's a whole pile of watches on top of the display case and they were deciding how many of each and, of course, Oscar steps in and starts to muscle in on the sale."

"What a fucker." Salvador bit his lip, brushing away a noisy fly. His intestines writhed and growled. "Gabi, I really don't see how you can put up with that shit. You shoulda quit when Luisito did."

"Wait!" The hand shot up again. "I still haven't told you how this man conducted himself." Gabi tried to draw in great breaths of air through his nose. "Oscar walks right over behind the case where I'm standing and says to the Colombians, 'In what can I help you, señores?' I just stood there and stared at him. As if I were invisible!" He grabbed some tissue and violently blew his nose, which was by now pink and swollen.

Salvador's ulcer began to bite him as he pictured Oscar. When he passed his eyes over Gabi, Salvador thought of how the boys in the labor camp in Texas would harass and bother him. His own light skin, hair and eyes, were quite a contrast to Gabriel's sallow, drawn face and hairy body. Always together, they were easy targets. A smile formed on his lips when he thought of the two of them, youths, alone in Miami amidst the others "unclaimed" in the chaotic Tent City under the highway. It was a tribute to their luck, del Cubano as they say, that they had both been sent to Texas.

They had been together almost five years now. His partner's stooped form caused Salvador to sigh loudly. Then the drawn face turned up. The whites of Gabi's eyes were flooded and veined. How could anyone do anything but love this man? He swiped at a fly before stretching his hands over in order to stroke Gabi's hairy arms.

Gabi sniffed some more, an uneven smile breaking on his lips. "You know, the commission would have been about three hundred dollars. We could have sent those medicines to your grandmother. Imagine Salvador, we could have . . ."

Salvador's eyes widened. Angel, he said to himself, here he is thinking about my grandmother in Cuba and probably the calls too. Salvador got off the stool and went into the kitchen to kiss Gabi's forehead, then caressed his closely cropped mustache.

"Don't worry yourself about abuela. We just sent her the last package in June. How long has it been? My love," he raised Gabi's face in his hands, "only four months have passed! She can't really expect us to be sending medicines all the time." Salvador took the wet hands in his as if making a vow. "Now, really Gabi, I seriously want to you think about quitting."

"You know what he said to them, right in front of me? Laughing, he said, 'Let me take care of you, sirs. This mariquita doesn't know anything about quality watches.' Can you believe it? Can you believe it? I swear, Salvador, I was so angry I could have spit in his face."

Some moments passed. The timer rang, announcing that the rice was done, and the air conditioner adjusted itself back down. Gabi had gone to the bathroom and Salvador was chewing on an antacid when he returned. They were apart again when Salvador asked what the Colombians had said. He was rolling his shoulders that were stiff with tension, but the fly was still buzzing about, so he folded up some newspaper instead and waited for it to light.

"I think they were as shocked as I was. But that's not all; I hadn't finished. Oscar pushes away all the watches they had definitely picked, pulls out some expensive Swiss ones and says 'Now these are quality watches, not that Taiwanese trash.'" Gabi imitated his boss's gestures and speech. He blew his nose again. "Needless to say they walked right out." Salvador smashed the paper against the windowpane and the fly slid onto the sill, immobile.

"What did you tell him?" Salvador sat down again shaking his head and tugging on the dozen or so strands of blonde hair at the nape of his neck then stuck another tablet in his mouth.

"Nada, what am I gonna tell him? 'You shiteater. You just lost me the biggest sale I would've had in months?' Nada, I didn't tell him anything." Gabi threw another rumpled wad of tissue into the garbage. He turned his eyes downward. "But the worse part is the way he made me look in front of them."

Salvador rubbed his stomach and burped. "I can't allow you to go back there, Gabi. One thing is for him to be a comemierda, but it's quite another thing to be humiliating you like that. It's just not right."

"Sí, Salvador, pero," Gabi said slowly, taking sighs between phrases, "I've been there so long and I finally got the raise he had promised me after Luisito left. Dios mío, I just don't know what else to do. Where could I go? The rest of the stores on Lincoln Road pay less and they're always getting robbed. No se, Salvador. No se que hacer."

Salvador's feet were tapping wildly under the counter. Then he jumped up. "Ya! I will not permit that beast to speak to you in that way. You won't go back. That's it! Let him stay there all day by himself watching over his fucking merchandise." His cheeks were bright red while Gabriel's were bloodless. He waved his arms about while pacing. "Don't make yourself crazy, Gabi. I'll find you something downtown—near me. Tomorrow, we'll go down there together." Gabriel came around and they locked arms; their slim bodies pushing together. After some moments,

Gabi fingered Salvador's bare chest and asked if he needed his medicine. They both laughed as Salvador clutched his stomach.

The next day they left the apartment a half hour early so that Gabi could be introduced to Salvador's bosses, Mr. and Mrs. Betancourt. They sent him over to an electronics store on Second Avenue owned by their in-laws, the Guzmáns. There was a loud speaker over the door blasting salsa music onto the sidewalk. The display windows were completely filled with all sorts of cheap gadgets, large and small battery-operated toys, rainbow-colored radios, portable tape players and it seemed to Gabi that there were at least thirty different types of calculators.

The Guzmáns wouldn't give him more than twenty hours a week and these only at minimum wage, but Gabriel took it anyway and told them that in the mean time he would keep looking. He had never had a job in Cuba. Too young to work, he just attended the Politécnico. Gabi didn't know what kind of job was his ideal one. He didn't know where and in what he worked best and he didn't know where to look either.

Business was often brisk in the mornings. When there weren't any customers in the store, Gabi dusted all the display items, swept behind the showcases, washed the windows, and organized the storeroom. The few times he was able to browse through the merchandise were when Mr. Guzmán went to the bank and Doña Lucy (as Mrs. Guzmán liked to be referred to) was not in the store so that just Gabi and their nephew, David, were left taking care of business. Gabi was most amused by the telephones; they entertained and distracted him. The store stocked phones in all colors, brands, sizes and bizarre shapes. There were lips, a sneaker, a hamburger, catsup and soda bottle telephones, a football phone, animals of all sorts—he liked the floppy-eared dog and mallard duck best. There was one in the form of a woman too.

By the end of the first month, Gabi was thoroughly disgusted with the store and his employers. But, as always, he kept it to himself, lest he worry Salvador. Pobre Dodo con su úlcera, he thought, he was already agitated enough. What with his family and their own money problems, Gabi tried to ease Salvador's mind as much as possible because he didn't want his stomach to get any worse.

Gabi re-counted the cash in his bank envelope on the bus ride home. At least it's under the table, he said to himself. Gabi's money was used for the groceries, so he regularly stopped at the Cuban bodeguita on the way back to the apartment to get fresh items for that night's supper. They had cancelled the cantina since he quit his job, so now besides the laundry and food shopping, Gabi did the cooking too. It was clear to both of them that he was the one who had more time; they had agreed and really, he didn't mind. Salvador would do the same for me, he told himself.

In the courtyard of the apartment building, Gabi noticed the blue and white phone bill jutting out of their mailbox. It was hot, very sunny and especially humid. There was no hint of a breeze to meet him as he went up the open-air stairs and corridor; he shook his head at the itemized calls. Seven to Cuba this time. Damned thing does not get below two hundred dollars a month! After unwinding the jalousie windows open to let the thick air out of the stuffy apartment, he placed the bill on the counter and tossed the junk mail before putting away the few groceries.

Gabi dropped two aluminum-wrapped tamales in a pot full of water to boil and began the picadillo. Tomato paste, ground beef, cooking wine, some capers, Spanish olives were gathered around the range while a chopped onion sizzled in oil. He diced up bits of potato and boiled them separately in a little tin pan. The rice cooker was already set and waiting for him to turn it on. A salad, he asked himself. Nah, there are still some string beans from last night, he answered himself, stirring in all of the ingredients except the potato.

Gabi left the beef cooking in its juices. The smell carried into the bedroom where he was changing into shorts and a sleeveless undershirt. Qué humedad, he sighed, wiping away the perspiration coating his neck and face. Gabi didn't like to switch on the air-conditioner until just before Salvador got home. Half an hour was usually enough time to sufficiently cool the small apartment. It's at least something he can do to save money. Oh, I forgot the salt, Gabi remembered. He slipped on thick rubber thongs that slapped the backs of his feet as he rushed towards the aroma-rich kitchen. He lowered the heat on the tamales and covered the pot, then drained the potatoes and spooned them into the picadillo after sprinkling it all with a bit of salt.

This phone bill is going to make some problems for us, Gabi contemplated. Salvador's car had needed tires last week and the cheapest they could find were recaps but even though a friend of a friend had given them a good price, they still came out to $100. Their little cache of savings was all but gone. That Disney World vacation they had intended for their fifth anniversary was indefinitely postponed. Salvador had said he would make it up to him and Gabi knew he would. He always did. Either by the way he looked when he first woke up, Chinese-eyed, pouting, his stylish hair all a mess, and baggy drawstring pajamas with his piss-hardened penis pointing the way to the bathroom. Or by his quick gestures of affection—a kiss, caress, or touch.

There was also something else, something very special to him. Gabriel loved to look at Salvador's face as he talked with his sisters or grandmother when they called. Gabi began to antici-pate the weekly collect calls with more anxiety than Salvador expressed. He still couldn't decide what it was in those hazel eyes that excited him; whatever it was, Gabi always stayed nearby to watch as his partner talked or listened. Perhaps it was the animation Salvador's face took on. Maybe it was just the tone of his voice; one he didn't use with him. Sometimes Gabi thought it was related to Salvador's being so different from him. A jealously of sorts. He occasionally wondered to himself if the emotion wasn't just that Salvador had *them*. Alguna familia.

Over and over Gabi thought about his watching of Salva-dor. Was it due to his temperament? He considered himself shy, preferring the shadows that Salvador's light gave.

Even when they were at the camp in Texas, Gabi avoided the group gatherings in the evenings and stayed away from the crowded television area, spending his time writing many let-ters home to Cuba, to his aunt Delia. Gabi had begun again to think about her of late. Although she never returned any of his letters, he hoped everything was all right. Gabriel had to make Salvador understand that she couldn't possibly write back. That might make her lose face with the Party. Gabi didn't want Delia to risk the privileges she had as a member. As he was stir-ring and tasting the meat, Gabi remembered just then that he had dreamed of her. Last night or when was it? What was it? The balcony of their apartment in La Vieja Habana. A soldier below, through the rusted iron railings. Was Delia interceding? Salvador wasn't there; or was he? He couldn't have been; they met here in Miami. Gabi covered the pan and turned it off. He unplugged the rice cooker and sat down trying to retrieve more pieces of the dream.

Was it a pair of soldiers? Gabi closed his eyes. He saw the narrow cobblestone streets, lined with balconies but he couldn't remember seeing any people in them, only himself and he wasn't a little boy. It was unusually quiet for the city. Delia was there, somewhere. Across the street? And he, he was, could he have been? Holding his penis, like a little boy. Urinating over the bars, over the soldiers. It was not a dream. He was fifteen and arrested. Delia had lost face that time too, for she was his guardian. She went to get him at the station. They never talked about it afterwards. No need to. Almost lost her little clout that time. He didn't get to say anything to Delia when they took him to jail then, that first time. Yet this dream, for he had dreamed about it, distorted his recollection of it. In the dream he was trying to tell her. Had he really been home alone? Gabi still couldn't recall that part. Then again the time they came to take him to Mariel Harbor. *No, you cannot leave a note.* The neighbors probably told her all about it anyway. Gabriel pictured her coming back to the empty apartment and sighing, maybe crying a little. Wavy thick hair like his but plastered under a flowered kerchief and unlike him, her plump, full features would flush brightly. Of course, she could not answer his letters. Poor tía, he said out loud, I hope she is well.

Shit! Almost six. Gabriel jumped up, remembering to turn on the air-conditioner. It won't cool fast enough, damn it. He wound up the window cranks, clinking the panes shut. Then he folded the phone bill and re-stuffed it into its envelope. Of course, he said to himself, Salvador must keep in contact with his family. We will find the money. If I could talk to Delia, I would too.

"Mi madre, qué calor!" Salvador said as he let himself in the apartment. "You didn't put the chain on."

"I had my hands full of groceries; then I started putting them away." Gabi looked at his slightly raised fine brows. "I forgot, that's all. What's the matter?"

"Ah, one of those days." Salvador tossed his keys across the counter. They slid onto the floor. "Mierda."

Gabi sighed when Salvador passed by without attempting to kiss him. He tried to push the bill out of sight but Salvador glimpsed in its direction.

"Already? Coño, it seems like we just sent them money. We really should buy stock, don't you think?" He reached for the envelope.

Gabi turned to the steaming pots and re-stirred the picadillo. He scooped out a forkful "Toma."

Salvador started to push it away, but then took it after all. "Good?"

"Horrendous and delicious." Salvador made a face. "The bill and your picadillo." He pulled out his shirt and unbuttoned it.

Gabi was surprised he was taking it so lightly.

"Well, we can eat whenever you're ready."

"I'm not that hungry just yet. Damn, is it hot." The afternoon sunlight caused him to squint as he looked outdoors. "Maybe, I'll take a shower." He opened the refrigerator and poured himself some milk.

"That won't take away your thirst."

"I know. I just want some milk."

"It's not good for your ulcer, Dodo."

"I know, Gabi."

"Salvador, something is happening. What is it?" He placed the fork and lid down on the range.

"I don't know." He wiped away some perspiration from his face. "Mierda y más mierda. Any other bills arrive?" He kept tugging and fanning himself with the wrinkled cotton of his shirt.

"No, nothing else." Gabi preferred Salvador to get angry at the stupid bill instead of this. This was more dangerous. He cautiously raised a hand to Salvador's shoulder. Salvador shifted his weight.

"I'm sweated, Gabi. Don't touch me." His voice was cool and even.

"Bueno, take a shower then, so we can eat." Gabi folded his arms over his chest, rubbing his thin biceps.

"I am not going to eat and I am not going to take a shower. O.k.? Ya! Come tu and leave me alone."

Gabi flinched. Like a house of cards, he folded himself into a flat pile of a seeming indifference. All those cards on top of one another, crisp, sharp edges yet, each layer warming the other. There was nothing, then, that he could do. Just let him alone. "Fine," he said at last.

Salvador went into the living room and turned on the television. He watched first the English news station then the Spanish news. After these, he watched a Venezuelan soap opera he had no custom of watching.

Gabriel heard it all from the kitchen as he stared at his neatly served dinner. Fluffy rice mixed in with meat. A dish of string beans dressed with onions and vinegar. He took a long time opening the banana leaves that sealed the tamal. The woman who sold the cantinas also made the tamales and stuffed potatoes that Salvador loved as well. The corn meal was smoothly ground with hints of picante. The meat filling that sometimes remained cold and hard if not cooked long enough was warm and tasty.

As he was eating, Gabriel knew that even though it was good, the dinner would sit heavy on his stomach. He could not enjoy it. He ate more for his eyes than for his hunger. When he finished, he cleared and cleaned everything he used. The remaining meat, rice and tamal were left in their pots, ready for re-warming at a moment's notice, though Gabi doubted that Salvador would eat.

Gabi went to brush his teeth and heard the theme music from the novela they watched every night. He returned to the living room to sit at the edge of the sofa. "If you're going to eat, let me know so that I can warm it up or put it away."

"No quiero, Gabi. No tengo deseo de comer." Salvador did not look up.

"Está bien." Gabi's bony shoulders pointed outwards.

They watched the soap opera in silence. The supper formed a rock in Gabi's stomach. He got up once during a commercial to take a tablespoon of a chalky tonic that Salvador used for indigestion. It was eleven thirty when Gabi said he was going to lay down. Salvador didn't move, only nodded. He stayed next to the set flipping from channel to channel. He said, at last, that he would come to bed soon.

After undressing, Gabi lay down with his eyes wide open,

rubbing his flat belly. For a while he thought of the bill, Delia, the store. He knew that once he was asleep, Salvador would come to bed. In the morning it would be like nothing. He'd come back from the bathroom, still rigid and perhaps they would make love. He was always repentant in the morning; the sun streaming through the yellow curtains, the chilly room, the dreamy baby talk. And Gabi always forgave him.

ABUELA MARIELITA

MY DAUGHTER DOESN'T want people to know that I came through the port of Mariel so she tells them that I came by way of Spain in January 1980, four months before I actually arrived en los cayos.

In the beginning, Gertrudes and Miguel didn't care, the first year it was fine to say that I came on a boat not a jet, something I've never done. I used to like to tell people about the nice young man who took me and the others on his speedboat, such an enchanting boy, so happy that the guards had found his aunt and uncle, his only family left in Cuba. He said he didn't care that we others weren't parientes of his as long as Chelita y Tatín were on the boat, although he had tried to find a sister of one of his neighbor's, her name was Ester Ramírez. I remember because I went to school with an Ester Ramírez, but that's all, just three people were on his list. Ah, que muchacho más bueno.

He had been in Mariel Harbor waiting four days when his tíos were brought to the pier, imagine, not knowing if they would be able to go and all. I rode on the bus with them though I didn't know them at the time, of course. I was staying with my cousin's son and his wife in a section of the house I used to own before the revolution and Jorgito, that's my prima's son, was making arrangements to get on the list to leave. Well, if they were leaving I wasn't going to be of any use to anyone. My mother died when I was pregnant and her only living brother went to Santiago with his wife's family. I didn't have any parientes left in La Habana, so what did I have to stay for? My daughter was in Miami and my son José Angel died as a young man in Playa Girón, so I had no reason to stay in Cuba at all. Oh, I wanted to be with my daughter so much, pobrecita, after so many years, she didn't have anyone in Miami.

It's true that Miguel's family is very large but that day Jorgito said that I had to decide right away and I did. I slept on it and prayed to the Virgins (both la Caridad del Cobre and Nuestra Señora de las Mercedes—one of my namesakes) to help me and they did. In three days some guards came to the house to get me, by then Jorgito y Lola were gone, poor things, God knows where they ended up. I gave him my daughter's address, but I've never heard anything from him. I believe his wife had some family in Tampa but Gertrudes says that's very far from Miami although I know it's still in Florida because I found it in one of my granddaughter's books when I was cleaning her room.

Well, anyway, after the first year or so, there were so many of us here and it was not popular to help Marielitos anymore. Things got very bad. One day I was darning some of my son-in-law's socks in the Florida room towards the rear of the house and I heard a big boom! My heart almost stopped; I thought it was a bomb but it was the front door that had been knocked down. Right in the middle of broad daylight, there was this big empty moving truck parked right on the lawn and two men standing there ready to steal everything in the house. Qué descarados! I yelled at them and they just calmly got back into their truck and drove away. Of course, I was very frightened. That's when Gertrudes and Miguel decided to move from la Pequeña Habana out to Westchester. That's also when they told me not to say anything about being an exile from Mariel. My daughter won't even let me speak about it in front of my grandchildren Marcos y Graciela either, though I'm sure la niña knows something because she was already talking when I arrived but even she doesn't say anything. She speaks non-stop English anyway; I can hardly understand her sometimes. The little one, Marcos, has no idea of course; he'll be six soon.

My yerno, Miguel, owns a glass store on Flagler Street, the Cristalería Siboney, and Gertrudes works in an office for the county—a very good job with benefits for her, Miguel and the children. I go to the Cuban clinic for the doctor because her insurance doesn't cover me but I don't mind because I see so many of my friends there especially now when I go every week for my terápia—my wrist feels much better. I twisted it while pulling Marcos away from the American man's dog next door. The dog had the ball Marcos threw over the fence in its mouth and the child was trying to pull it out and through the fence. Well, the dog wanted to play too but children can be so bad sometimes; thanks to God, the boy is fine. After that, Miguel put up a wooden fence that blocks the view of the other neighbors' yards, a shame because Josefina and her husband have such lovely gardenia bushes and the neighbors's patio to the rear of us, the López's, has banana and papaya plants that remind me of my own patio in Cuba. When I was newly married and my mother was still alive, I used to grow jazmínes and dalias in the courtyard, I haven't seen any dalias here though.

The new house my daughter and son-in-law bought has an

apartment in the back; actually it's a little room but I guess for one person it's fine. A few months after we had moved here and all the neighbors got to know us (and not know too much about me, of course) the room was rented to an older señora. She kept me company sometimes during the day while I took care of the children and, Lord knows, I could use Ofelia's, that's her name, help. Ese Marcos es un ciclón! Gracielita is no saint, either. Pobrecita Ofelia, what a kind soul, she couldn't take care of herself after a while, kept falling down and not being able to get back up, so her sons, God forgive them, put her in one of those homes where they are supposed to take care of old folks. She was only six or seven years older than me and I'm 72. She was such a good listener too.

I meant to talk about Yamile and maybe I steered away from the subject at times but forgive me because I'm an old woman. Yamile came through Mariel also and moved into the cuartico behind the house after Ofelia left. She was very fat for such a young woman, so my daughter didn't notice that she was pregnant although I could tell by her look almost immediately; it was the look of a woman with child. Miguel wanted to kick her out when he found out, but Luz, the baby, sleeps almost all night, so he cannot complain too much; besides with the windows closed, you can't hear a thing anyway. Gertrudes doesn't like Yamile and treats her very rudely, something I lament very much because I have come to care for her and the baby, poor things.

At first, Gertrudes did not mind that I was talking to Yamile, although sometimes she made little comments about Yamile and her being on welfare and only working part-time at the farmacia near us. But then again, she couldn't say too much because Yamile always pays her rent on time and in full. She doesn't know, of course, that I give her a little hand with my food stamps ever since they gave me more. I never told my daughter that I get $60 and not $40—I'm always here when la cartera comes; we have a woman to deliver the mail, isn't that something? Nice girl. Plus, whenever they give out cheese or powdered milk, I always give Yamile some. She needs it much more than we do and my grandchildren don't eat that cheese. They like the store-bought wrapped squares better. Anyway, Miguel has his own business that is doing well and my daughter makes a good salary. I shouldn't even be taking the stamps but my daughter says they pay taxes for them and we might as well take them. I don't say anything about it anymore.

Yamile has been living here for almost a year now and Luz is just a little doll. I spend a lot of time with her now that both of the children are going to San Bernardo's. To me, Luz is like my own grandchild because I've been with her since birth. Yamile leaves her with me in the mornings when she goes to work. Most of the time the baby just sits and plays in the crib while I prepare the dinner or fold the clothes. She doesn't talk yet so we haven't cut her hair; it's long in the back but kind of thin on top, angelita, she'll look better when it all grows in.

In the morning when it's still not so hot, after everyone's gone, Luz and I go to the patio to hang up the clothes. She watches from that baby swing Marcos used to love so much. My daughter was throwing it out before I stopped her. I hang the clothes because I really don't like to use the clothes dryer. It's so much better to sun the things and let them blow in the breeze; they smell so much nicer too. Gertrudes finally stopped fussing about it when Miguel said that they would save on the electricity. They spend so much already with the air conditioners on from the time they walk in the door until they leave the next day. I always turn them off (they have five!) when they're gone and open all the windows; I don't even sleep with the one in my room on though my daughter can't understand. The fan is really just fine for me; I tell her that the air conditioner gives me a sore throat. The children know how to turn them on and it's the second thing they do, after they turn on the television, the minute that bus drops them off and they run through the door. I only like to watch my novela in the evening; it's the same one my daughter watches so I can watch it on the big screen. I'd really rather listen to the radio during the day though. It seems that the television is on almost as much as the air conditioner sometimes and of course, la niña has her own little color t.v. in her room. Marcos is starting to ask for another one, so my son-in-law promised him a color set for his birthday if he brings home a good report card this term. I don't understand but I don't say anything because he is their father and I don't want him to say that I meddle, like I heard him say one time when I was going to bed. Anyway, Luz and me, we hang the clothes together and sometimes I'll sing to her, she's such a happy baby. I'm enjoying her much more than I did Marcos because I was always worrying about what Gracielita was doing the minute I turned away, what a child, that one, always into everything. I'm sure half my gray hairs belong to her.

It was a very hard thing for me to find Yamile in the condition she was in when I went to take her a plate of food from Marcos's fifth birthday party. They had set up the patio with rented chairs and tables and there were trays and trays of pasteles Cubanos filled with guayaba, queso y carne; sandwichitos of sweet ham with jelly and cheese or a creamy meat paste—I love those. And they ordered a huge blue and white sheet cake with those little robots, the cartoon ones that Marcos watches all the time; he has them all over the house. His parents got him a piñata in the shape of one of them, oh, what does he call them? Something of el universo, I don't remember now, but he even had a costume for that fiesta the North Americans have in October. Bueno, I'll remember it later. There was music and all of the neighbor families were invited; even the man from next door, Miguel said we had better invite him or he would call the police about the music which was way too loud because Gracielita and her amiguitas would change to an American station and turn up the volume whenever they got the chance, though they never did dance to it anyway.

There were so many people there besides the neighbors' children and kids from San Bernardo's. There was Miguel's family from Hialeah, all of them. Even a first cousin of his that came via Mariel, but he didn't say anything to her, imagine, not even hello. There were a couple more North Americans too from my daughter's job though they left right away after we cut the cake. Probably got bored talking to themselves; the neighbor man left early too. It was already in the evening when people were serving themselves more arroz con pollo. By then it had cooled off too and oh, there were tamales too and I made a big aluminum tray of potato and chicken salad. I spelled Marcos' name on top with pimento slices but he never saw it. He was too busy riding around all afternoon on the bicycle that Miguel bought him or running in and out of the house showing friends the new game tapes he got for his t.v. even though Gertrudes told him not to bring kids into the house. They didn't stop until they broke one of her Lladro figurines; she has a whole vitrina filled with them. It took me three pots of café to serve everyone, it's a good thing Ofelia left me hers, so I only had to wash one right away to make more for the last two people. Everyone seemed satisfied, either rubbing their bellies, sipping espresso or going back for more food, so I thought I'd check in on Yamile and Luz.

The music was still too loud but I could hear the baby. Luz was very little then, maybe three months, I could hear her crying above all the noise. Gertrudes was talking with Estrella from across the way, poor woman, her son killed himself with drugs, only sixteen years old, a sad thing, really. Hemm, ah sí. I think Miguel went for more ice or beer or both though I can't imagine what was taking him so long; he slips away a lot lately but I've learned to bite my tongue about it. Marcos was playing computador with his friends and Gracielita was shut up in her room with two or three girls. They were talking on the phone when I checked in on them; I don't like it when she locks that door like that. Anyway, she did something that upset me very much. She's gotten such a mouth since starting school at San Bernardo's. I asked las muchachitas if they wanted any more soda, in Spanish of course, but Gracielita answered me in English with that face she puts whenever she's acting up and they all laughed. All I could understand her saying was something about me being a Marielita but I'm sure it was worse than that. I would have slapped her right then and there but my daughter doesn't believe in that, so I called her a fresh and shameless girl and they kept right on laughing. Such disrespect! I was so angry, I just wanted to shake her but the only thing I could do was close the door hard behind me. Marcos saw me in the hall and called out for more soda so I brought some back for him and his friends. None of them said thank you. Gertrudes asked me if the children were all right when I walked passed the living room. I said yes and went to my room to get my fan; my face was on fire! I took an extra tranquilizer from my drawer and remembered Yamile and the baby; her room shares a wall with my bedroom.

Well, when I passed the living room to go to the kitchen, Gertrudes asked me for more café and I told her I would get it in a few minutes. She said she wanted some now with the cake she was eating and I told her to make it herself or wait for me and walked right on by to the kitchen for the chicken and rice I left in the oven for Yamile and then back to the tables in the yard and got some salad and a few pastelitos. Of course, Gertrudes would wait but I could see through the sliding door that she was raising some fuss about it with that conceited Hortensia; she's always talking about Spain trying to catch me up in the lie but I always say I can't remember the names of places in Madrid. Anyway, I got together a nice heaping serving for Yamile and I decided to put a big piece of cake on a separate plate because there was so much of it left. It had much too much merengue— even for me—and the children didn't like the pineapple filling so more than half the cake was left even though there must have been close to a hundred people there at one point or another. I figured I'd bring Yamile cake later so I took the plate which had those universo robots printed on it—the napkins, cups and paper tablecloths all matched too. I managed to save one of the cake decorations for Luz, I felt it in my pocket against my waist then, hands full, I walked around to Yamile's little room behind the utility shed where the washer and dryer are.

Angel of God, to remember that poor girl with that whimpering baby, ay, it just breaks my heart. It's always very hot in that part of the house and there wasn't a single breeze. Pobrecita, she only has two windows in that little room and facing the east so all she gets is hot air. She was drenched and fanning herself and the baby with a piece of cardboard. Luz was kicking around and bright red. I could tell that her sheets were all sticky too. I noticed that there was a plate of bread and I think mayonesa on the table next to the crib. But that's all! Yamile got up right away and told me to sit but I put the food before her and made her stay put. She always calls me doña Soledad; she's the only one who's ever called me by my first name. Most everyone calls me Mercedes, but I have always liked Soledad because it was my mother's name and it reminds me of her; my full name's Soledad de las Mercedes Pérez y Pérez, not including my husband's name—Aguirre. Yamile's eyes were full of veins and she was in tears when she asked me what more she could do with Luz. I asked her how much she had fed her already; poor thing couldn't nurse because of the gland medicine she takes. She showed me two bottles that were still dirty with milk. I reached over and picked Luz up feeling the dampness of the mattress and the baby clothes and realized that I had never seen her drinking water. I turned right around bouncing Luz on my hip and called out, what that baby needs is water! Yamile's thin eyebrows arched up while I went on. You young people never ask the old ones anything because you know it all already. She was smiling and crying at the same time and then tears fell from my eyes, too while I prepared a fresh bottle of water. I held Luz close to my bosom as she drank while Yamile was eating the food from the party and watching us.

A FRACTION OF ALWAYS

DAMARYS WAS ALONE, driving from the west coast back to Miami on Alligator Alley, the cellular unusually quiet allowing her time to think. She was completing the arrangements her mother wanted—cremation, no funeral. She wanted to honor and celebrate her with an elaborate tomb, like those in Cuba's Colón, but given Mima's specific instructions, she felt obliged to comply. In life, her mother had not required her to comply, whether it was her mother's or her own personality, she didn't venture to guess now. It didn't matter now.

She was used to arranging everything for the family. For her mother's exile, there had been a faked vacation cruise from Cuba to Jamaica, political asylum, a very short stint in the Krome Avenue Detention Center. Mima had joked about her pleasant incarceration, the nice guards, how even the orange jumpsuit became her. Damarys had prepared a room especially for Mima in her, by then, third house, painting the walls a Caribbean blue, the color of Mima's santo, Yemayá, furnished with a solid mahogany bedroom suite, the four poster bed adorned with the softest down comforter and eyelet covered pillows, and, of course, the spacious walk-in closet (the size of her room in Cuba) stocked with fine multicolored ladies' dresses—the still-attached tags made it look like a store. Mima had loved that.

"And what if they don't fit me?" she had said, sweeping her hand across the rack, the plastic wraps swayed.

"We'll throw them away and buy some more," Damarys had replied.

"No!" First, there was a horrified look and then the mischievous smile. "We'll sell them!"

Damarys had laughed at her ignorance of American consumerism. "No, Mima, I can return them—for no reason—and get all my money back. It's not a problem."

That was an especially happy year. Damarys had orchestrated her brother's exile and asylum just months after Mima was settled. She knew, of course, that Fito couldn't be happy without Gabriela and Gogi, their son, her only nephew; but getting them out was more complicated by then. The politics in this country baffled her; while the president was a Democrat, exile had been easier, traveling there was easier and yet once the Republicans, who claimed to love the Cuban cause, got power it became harder for Cubans over there and here. Visiting the island had become an elaborate, extended game of chess. But with the tenacity of a pit bull, she had arranged her sister-in-law's exile, though it took almost three years. By some blissful stroke of luck, Gabriela's parents won the Cuban exit lottery, receiving permission to "abandon their patria" and were here not long after.

No one left in Cuba except her sister-in-law's more distant relatives but they were deeply entrenched in the Party, so had little interest in coming. But if Gabriela really wanted them, Damarys would figure out a way to get them here too. Damarys always figured things out; she had arranged for the sleek forty foot cigarette to pick them up at Guanabo beach—at $5,000 per person—and speed them across the straits onto land because of the wet foot, dry foot policy. She, Yarely in her arms, Misael, and Solimar emerged from the shallow blue-green water into exile. When they stepped onto the beach on Key Biscayne, only the slightly interested tourists looked up from their mats. She and Misael loved to call themselves speedboat balseros—no sunburn, dehydration, sharks or rafts for them.

Tía Nena, Mima's older sister who'd lived in Miami for many years, was mystified as to how they could gather the $20,000 American dollars when most Cubans made $10 to $15 a month. Damarys didn't go into detail with Tía Nena but made her understand that it took a whole lot of hustling and then let drop that they were especially lucky running a numbers business. Drumming her acrylic nails on the steering wheel, without design or embellishment now out of respect for her mother, Damarys recalled her first stateside phone call to Tía.

"It's Damarys, Tía Nena. We've arrived," she was excited to hear her aunt's voice.

"Yes, yes, of course, I was expecting to hear from you," she paused. "Your mamá called me last week. I was worried. Are you all together, all right?"

"Yes, Tía, thank God, it was an easy passage. We went through the processing and paperwork and now we're staying with Misael's brother in Homestead." Damarys could hear her aunt coughing a little.

"In Homestead? So far? That's more than an hour from me," she paused again. "What will you do?"

"Don't worry, Tía." Her question implied both that she felt some obligation and that she would not be of much help. Damarys wondered if her aunt thought she would have to claim them. "We'll go to see you as soon as we get our bearings—is that all right, Tía?"

"Oh, I didn't mean . . . You know I would love to see you all. I just hate driving long distances by myself anymore. John and I don't ever go down to Miami."

Almost a dozen years had passed since that phone call, providing Damarys with some perspective on her aunt's reticence. Driving to Miami now she was struck by the irony; Damarys had never counted on help from anyone before or since.

Tía Nena had left Cuba so long ago that she really did not comprehend how it was for them back there. No idea about the daily, tedious struggle for food. Nobody starved in Cuba; there weren't hyper extended bellies or fly infested lost gazes of children. But people were always hungry. Her ration book allowed a quarter chicken per family member per month, five lbs of rice though it was later cut back to three lbs, ten lbs of sugar that everyone used to make wine or liquor to drink or sell. Beans were the staple protein for so many years that children growing up in the revolution didn't know that a traditional Cuban meal was accompanied by a side of rice and beans and plantains but always featuring some meat as the main course. But that was before Fidel.

She hustled everyday to find fish or chicken for her children—beef was impossible to find or pay for; once every two or three months, Misael would go to a farm just outside the city for a pig. The trick was getting it to their apartment without detection, Jorge, el guajiro, had already cut its vocal cords so as to keep the noise down. Tía didn't know about the pigeons Fito kept on the roof for soups and stews until Gogi grew so attached to the birds that his heart-wrenching sobs forbade us to kill any more. Mima and Tía communicated by periodic letters, notes really because Tía wasn't particularly expressive; usually only mundane details with occasional news of a graduation or engagement and photos rarely—it was hard to tell that way if some of Tía's letters ever went astray. Tío Edi, the oldest of the siblings, had gone through Mariel with Tía Luisa and her cousins Luisita and Elena. They had all lived through the various "special" periods, each more difficult than the previous one. He and Tía Nena only got to spend five years together en la yuma, in the US; he was sick most of it with cancer. Only the sisters were left. Well, now only Tía. A tightness gripped her throat. *Ay, Mima, what do I do?* She cried a little in answer to her own question.

When they were in Cuba, Mima could count on her sister to send Christmas money every year, which arrived via telegraph from Spain. Damarys was grateful and respectful of her aunt but it was out of obligation to Mima that she called her every other week when they first came to Miami. To her, Tía was distant, Americanized. Maybe it was because she had married the American John, she could not bring herself to call him Tío, though he looked more Latino than Tía with his Mediterranean skin and wavy black hair. Their sons didn't speak Spanish either and had gone off to the north to study with no intention of moving back maybe because Tía and John had sold their family house and bought a small condo in Hollywood. Damarys knew that it was considered normal for Americans but it seemed to her that parents in this country were putting their children out. Maybe she was backwards that way; who knew, maybe Tía had it right but she didn't understand the logic or see the advantage.

There was a large gray gator sunning on the canal bank on her right, nothing but dry grasses, scrub oak and palmetto on her left, an occasional sign announcing the miles left to the end of the most desolate part of the drive across the state. No cell signal, no calls, just the smooth steady engine hum of the pricy German sedan which she had bought for Mima though she had flat out refused it.

"I don't even have a license, Dary," she said, handing the keys back.

"No matter, who's going to stop you? If you really want one, we'll get you the license," Damarys answered, dangling the keys before her.

"Hija, don't you see, I can't be bothered, after all, I have you to resolve all my problems, verdad?"

"Pues claro, mami, always."

But it wasn't even a fraction of always. Damarys thought about the time it took to gather the resources to make it all happen, to bring her mother to her side, enjoy her and allow her to enjoy her granddaughters growing up with American conveniences and privileges. Mima only had that pleasure and comfort for six short years. She had supervised the girls' driving lessons, chaperoned them to parties or after school activities— her girls were never unattended—another point of contention with American child rearing—why was it that children here were left alone so much? Mima was in the front pew when first Solimar got married and then, last summer, for the hurry-up wedding of 17-year-old Yarely to 16-year-old Javi. In the end, Solimar produced the first great-grandchild for Mima and she got to rejoice in many of the baby's firsts; she could explicitly recount Betty's first smile, her laughter, the way she pinched her ears and bounced on her belly. Mima was there so vividly and for so much. She was the first one to cross the threshold into their custom built house of houses—seven bedrooms, seven bathrooms, three kitchens (Mima's favorite was the outside one). She loved the wrought iron balconies overlooking the courtyard and could not believe the gleaming marble floors were so easy to clean though she complained so much about the water drops in the front entry caused by the wall length water-fall that they kept it turned off. Of course, there were not all wonderful things; the hepatitis she got in Cuba became sclerosis of the liver once here. There were many doctors, specialists, but no one could change the diagnosis and her rapid decline, a fraction of a fraction of always. Mima had been admitted to the hospital last Saturday when she was too uncomfortable to walk or even sit.

"Mija, I can't anymore," she said, frozen in a painful contortion. "Take me to the hospital."

By Wednesday, she had slipped into an unreachable state. There was nothing more to do for Mima in this life. She didn't want to be intubated either, another explicit instruction. Her stout body and elegant face, even her lovely hands, were finally unrecognizable. Now there was an insurmountable void.

Damarys couldn't imagine her life without Mima. How difficult it had been to live for eight long though busy years without her, the time it took to accumulate the wealth and to advantageously position her family. Gabriela's parents wanted nothing to do with the business but Damarys had even arranged for her own father, Mima's estranged though still friendly first husband, to run one of their small operations. Damarys was proud of herself because she had succeeded, like real Americans;

she knew how to take care of business. They had bought and sold properties, become landlords, established first a successful trucking company, then various other illegitimate though incredibly lucrative businesses that required all of her chispa and newly claimed Yankee, as well as innate, Cuban ingenuity. She recalled the nights their first year here when she was a security guard patrolling the parking lots of the twenty-four hour warehouse while Misael was transporting new Mercedes norte on the semi—ten at a time, for $500 a piece. Because there was no one she trusted to leave the girls with, they slept in the patrol car as Damarys drove around. It's true, she thought to herself, they had worked like animals in this country, and though in Cuba they were used to hustling, the level required here was unlike anything they had previously encountered. There everyone hustled; it was the only way, the Cuban way, after Fidel and maybe before too. It was what one did to resolver, to solve problems. Here there was respite from the intensity of assuring survival, but she had discovered early on that to dramatically improve one's lot here, to really move beyond the typical Miami-Cuban version of wealth— gold saint medallions and diamond-encrusted Rolexes, a fancy car or truck, a ridiculous mansion in the midst of a noisy, crowded sauguecera, Westchester or Kendall neighborhood—they had to make big deals, take greater risks. At one point a babalao client of theirs declared that they would achieve untold success if the whole family embraced Santería as initiates. While Damarys didn't practice, Mima had always believed, keeping her own little altar stocked with molasses, little candy fishes, flowers and water for "su virgencita, de Regla, como yo." But Damarys took the oath, shaved her head, wore white for a year and practiced with fervor. Misael said she looked liked a queen with her turban and was impressed with her new calm and increased power, but it was ultimately how much business *did* improve that convinced him to convert too. Then she became a babalao herself, a high priestess of Obatalá; people paid her tribute—another extra income. The girls reluctantly agreed though they only wore white when at home and there was no way they'd allow anyone near their scalps with shears, which was only excused because they were still virgins. Everything moved swiftly after that; deals struck and cash flowed, an unstoppable fountain of money. Damarys got her breasts lifted and her tummy tucked out of pure caprice. She decided to when she saw the Hummer ad on a South Miami billboard: Porque quiero, porque puedo y porque me gusta. She wanted to, had the money and liked the idea. In fact, she bought the Hummer too—she was assured it was the only white one in Florida—even before the surgery. These days she wore comfortable though expensive jeans and mostly managed the businesses, as Misael had to keep a low profile after the last run in with the law.

She was crossing the Everglades without delays—two hours from her house where she stopped to get the cash for the funeral parlor in Southwest Miami, glad that the wildfire smoke wasn't bad today despite a severe drought announced even on the Spanish language television. Her mother had joked about the water rationing guidelines, saying that Cubans couldn't be told to do anything after Fidel. Mima had commented about the effect of the dictator's long convalescence after almost dying—nada cambio—everything just the same. Damarys sucked her teeth. *That son of a bitch still alive and her poor mother dead and bloated with seventy-five lbs of fluid.* She wondered about the cell phone reception out there in the middle of the occasionally muddy and often nearly dry swamp, but a quick glance reassured her of the low though present signal. Come to think of it, she had not called too many people. Just Tía Luisa and her father who did her the favor to call Tía Nena who she supposed would call her cousins—not that they would show up or even call. She had mostly talked back and forth with the funeral home director after leaving the hospital, to confirm the flower orders and to make sure they would all be in place when the body was ready to be viewed for the 24 hour velorio, a Cuban style viewing—another instruction of her mother's. But Mima had left her one loophole—Damarys got to order as many flowers as she wanted. Mima loved bright flowers, especially miniature carnations and requested them, in life, not just for her saint but also for her own selfish pleasure.

"Promise me you'll always bring me fresh flowers, mija," she had said when they first picked her up at Krome Avenue almost six years ago as she deeply inhaled the two dozen roses the girls handed her.

"Siempre, Mima, you'll never lack them, I promise."

Damarys had made a special trip just two days ago to Miami to select the flower arrangements after the doctor told them there was nothing more they could do. How could she comprehend that there was no way to change the outcome, no bribe, trick or solution to this problem? She had to leave the hospital, even if it was for a few hours. Tía Nena had surprised her and had driven from Hollywood to the hospital by herself.

"Don't worry, I'll be here. Go, resolve the arrangements." Tía Nena's voice cracked.

"Tía, please stay with us tonight. It's a long trip for you . . ." She didn't finish.

"No, no, no, no. I'll go home tonight. I would be in the

way . . ." She couldn't finish.

"But Tía, how can you say that? You're family. We have plenty of room," Damarys was starting to feel her own voice crack.

"No, hija, no, don't worry. Whenever you return, I'll go. Let me be of use during this time," she said and raised her hand before Damarys could protest again.

"Bueno, I appreciate it. Mima's so far gone . . . I'm glad you'll be here."

Did she say, call me if . . . ? Did she assume Damarys would call her? No matter now. Tía, not Damarys, was there when the miracle happened. Mima awoke. For two hours, she sat up and chatted with her sister. It was as if they had visited each other every other week; neither one thought to call Damarys though coincidentally, Tía Luisa called Tía Nena's cell and was able to talk to her too. Later Luisa apologized for not calling her either but she recounted how Mima had laughed at her teasing, saying she stayed in the hospital only to get the young handsome doctors to touch her all over. How she would have given anything to hear her mother's laughter once more.

By the time she returned, Mima had descended again into unconsciousness. Damarys tried to listen to what happened while reconciling the impulse to scream.

"The last thing she said was that she was tired," Tía Nena reported. "She said she was going to sleep and she did, so soundly, so naturally."

Damarys held on to the bed rail while Tía gathered up her things to drive back home "before dark." She wanted to know why she had missed her mother's awakening; she wanted to ask her everything, know every single word she said but Tía was hurrying. Damarys' stifled scream was sealed by a heaviness spreading from her throbbing head. Slowly, she walked her aunt to the hospital room door. Though they both knew exactly the circumstances when they would see each again and soon, neither one could utter more than a weak "adios". That night Mima's liver failed, then her kidneys—dialysis was only able to remove five lbs of fluid. She left her body early the next morning. They were all gathered around, all helpless, suffering while watching her swell with the fluid that inevitably choked her heart.

Damarys had asked the florist to create identical baskets of white roses from the girls—their ribbons had to be the palest yellow and green with red lettering—A Mima, de tus queridas nietas. From the girls and their husbands, there were to be multicolored pastel rose standing sprays, not just the typical Cuban coronas with white gladiolas, but filled instead with peace and calla lilies and tiny blue carnations—white ribbons with lavender lettering—adorada abuela, te queremos. Three more standing sprays, seven feet tall, with matching arrangements below, tuber roses, daisies, more spring colored carnations, one for either side of the coffin from Misael and his family and a separate one from all of the grandchildren—de tus nietos. She felt compelled to order a four-foot wide broken heart, a red jagged line of roses dissecting the puffed white pillow of chrysanthemums; this one would be from Fito who was devastated by Mima's last breath, collapsing in a heap next to the hospital bed. She decided on a baby blue and pink wreath from Betty, the only great-grandchild—thanks to God I knew you, abuelita. To cover the casket, a spray of white roses with purple orchids. The last corona she ordered would be hers. A pure white standing spray of roses to tower over them all. White ribbon with blue glittering letters—Mima, always, Damarys.

THE FRESH BOYS

PAPO CALLED DOUGIE to catch a ride to school because it was raining like hell and he didn't feel like taking the city bus. Dougie's answering machine clicked on after three rings; Papo hung up and mumbled to himself. Six forty-five in the morning and this guy's already cruising the parking lot.

Papo's best friend and roommate, Manny, didn't have a car and was skipping school today so he didn't bother to wake him (Manny's parents were long gone to work in Hialeah so the apartment was empty). So he grabbed his baseball uniform and stuck it in a plastic grocery bag, doubting that the driving rain would stop in time for today's practice at three. Qué mierda, he said and reluctantly put on his cap to head out to school.

Dougie was pissed because he wouldn't be able to show off his new speakers to "the boys" in the parking lot so he contented himself by blasting the volume and driving around and around the school until the second bell rang. He had pulled the backseat out of his old VW bug to accommodate the speakers and now the bass made the car and his ears throb. Fucking rain, he banged his fist on the leather-wrapped steering wheel, can't even open the windows and they're all steamed up. Damned de-fogger never did work. When he saw the assistant principal at the front gate he considered it time to get to first period. Oh no, I didn't do the homework and today's a vocabulary test. What a shit.

Ray was early today but he didn't want to break his record so he stayed in the courtyard smoking a cigarette until he heard the tardy bell ring. He had already seen his girlfriend Debbie and they had agreed to skip school after lunch to go over to her house. Even though they had been having sex for a month now, they still couldn't wait until school let out at two-thirty to get into each other's pants. Some of his friends said hello to him through the crowds while others were opening and closing lockers, pulling books out as he thought of Dulce María. Ray really liked her, but she was Latin and wouldn't even let him feel her up so he had no hope of going to bed with her, which was something he thought about all the time now. He crushed the cigarette underfoot as the halls started to clear.

Ray met up with Dougie and Papo outside in the already flooding courtyard near the first period classroom. The rain continued to cascade down from the second floor storm gutters and spilled over the tiled walkways before the three of them. They were all marked absent and had to go to the attendance office in another building to get admit slips. The walk back to class took on a leisurely pace; they stuck their heads in open doors to call out names of friends, kicked lockers and tried to drown out the morning announcements by talking loudly in Spanish. After a while, the principal's voice came over the P.A. speakers to warn the student body against continued vandalism in the boy's locker room. Class work was delayed up and down the halls for more than ten minutes, but despite this, they came back in time for the vocabulary test. Miss Fernández gave them each a dittoed paper and told them to get to work.

Papo finished first and tilted his test sideways so that Dougie could see, but he was slumped over the desk sleeping so that the heavyset girl across from him looked up and past him.

"Don't cheat, Tracy," Papo said out loud. Miss Fernández came over and took their papers while the girl angrily protested.

Ray laughed and remarked in Spanish, "That broad is so stupid, man. I thought they were all smart." The other Spanish-speaking students—about half the class—laughed while the rest cursed under and over their breaths until the teacher finally said, "If I hear one more voice, you'll all get a zero on the test."

Dougie, startled by the noise, looked pleadingly at his classmates. "Shut up people, you're gonna get Miss Fernández mad."

After the class finished with the test, Miss Fernández wrote the homework assignment in light blue chalk on the board, underlining the due date in yellow. Some students grumbled in lowered tones while others copied.

Jay-Tee lifted her dreadlocks for a moment and asked the woman's back, "When is this due, Miss Fernandez?"

The teacher slowly turned around. "Why don't you finish copying and then ask me?"

Dougie got up and stood next to the woman's turned back eyeing her hips with raised eyebrows. Some of the class laughed and Miss Fernández swung around again.

"Sit down."

"But, Miss . . ."

"Sit down and wait until I'm finished."

Dougie strutted away and down the aisle with a wide grin

while the boys snickered. Papo leaned over to Ray and muttered in Spanish, "The homework I'd do with that body."

"No way, man. She's too gorda." Ray puffed his cheeks.

"Ah, you like them skinny American girls, bro. They don't have no meat." Papo turned up his cupped palms.

"They don't have lard, man."

Monica turned around and told them to shut up and they told her to go to hell. They had just begun to curse each other out when Miss Fernández interrupted them. "I'm only going to explain this once, so pay attention."

Bernard, by the back door, was inching his way out when Miss Fernández glanced up and he shot right down. She read from the board while some looked at their watches or put their pens down and away; others still were gathering their notebooks together and shifting in their seats. From the back of the room the tiny sound coming from a hidden headset tape cassette clicked on.

"O.k. This is your homework assignment which is due mañana—Tuesday. Tomorrow. Get it?"

"Yes, Miss Fernández, we heard you. We're not stupid, God!" Dougie said.

"All right, this is what you are going to do. Write your autobiography from childhood up to the present. You don't have to start with 'I was born on such and such a date at such and such a place.' Be creative. This should be a lot of fun."

There were scattered whines and groans around the room until Miss Fernández slammed a big dictionary down on her desk. She asked them if they were finished and began to talk again before they could reply. "It must be at least three pages long. Tell about the major events that have happened to you, what experiences you feel may have changed your life, talk about the most important people in your life and don't restrict yourself to your family members, o.k?" She looked around at them then asked, "Class, when is this due?"

They yelled out "tomorrow" and the second period bell rang, instigating a stampede.

It was still raining at the last bell when Dougie decided to go home to call his girlfriend because he didn't have enough gas to go to her house in Miami Springs today and last him the rest of the week. When he turned off the answering machine and put the receiver up to his ear, he cursed its high-pitched tone. Oh, man, don't tell me, he talked to it but the phone screeched on despite insistent jabbing of the button on his part. He finally slammed the receiver down and fell back on his bed, then looked at the t.v. set but didn't bother to get up and turn it on. Only thing on now is those stupid soap operas, ah, fuck it. I'll do homework. No! No! He shook himself a little but pulled some paper and a pen from his desk drawer anyway.

Let's see, he said, I guess I have to start with Cuba. He began to write. *I was born in La Habana on agosto 12, 1970.* Damn, I'll be eighteen this summer. His mind wandered a bit before taking up the pen again. *I can't tell you or I don't know if I can tell you what I feel about Cuba. Many times I don't no the right words. In Spanish or English.*

He read it over in his mind and thought some more before throwing it away and starting again. Major events, o.k. *I was 10 when I came here on a boat. I had many friends in school that were like me—(Marielitos).* He laughed at the word then repeated, Marielitos. I'm gonna freak her out. *They're here with me now in the high*

school. There are many gangs around now. We are the The Fresh Boys.
He printed this in big curved letters, the way they do with spray
paint and magic markers. *We were the Swamp Dawgs but some black
dudes from Overtown use that name so we changed.*

All right, born, came on a boat, school. O.k., more on that.
*I'm not as smart as my mother and father are. My mom works at a bank on
Brickell Avenue and my dad works downtown at the college.* He looked
out the window a moment and was surprised at the bright sun
drying the street. Naw, I gotta do this, he talked himself back
into writing. Mother . . . father, oh, right, family. *My father is a
geneus.* Naw, that don't look right, he scratched it out and started again. *My dad's really smart, he does interior designs and fabrics and. .
.* all that shit and *can draw really nice.* He underlined nice twice.

Dougie looked at his large, slanted script then added more
to the bottom of the page. *I like to draw but I can't do it like him.* Oh
yea, I forgot. He squeezed his letters to fit on the last line. *I'm an
only child. My name is Douglas because my father said it was some famous
designer's name.*

He read the first page over and when he got to the bottom
put a star before the last two sentences. He put another star at
the top and followed it down the page. I ain't gonna rewrite this
shit, still got two more to go. Oh, Miss Fernández, what a drag.
He got himself a glass of soda from the kitchen, forgetting to
check the phone. Sitting back down, he started on a new page.

Gotta go up to the present, so I'll tell about my fresh car. *I
bought a hot orange 1975 VW bug last. . .* He stared off to the poster
of a Lamborghini Countach, which took up most of the wall
over his bed, as he counted months on his fingers. Damn almost
a year, and then finished the sentence. *year. I put a chrome engine
in it.* He thought about the gringos' Camaros, Z-28's and Mus-

tangs in the parking lot. *I'm the only one in the whole school who has a chrome engine.* Dougie looked at the page and cursed, then spread out the letters and stayed far from the margins. *I took picture of it. It's really super nice.* Mierda y más mierda. *I like to go out and cruise on the weekends. I go with my boys down to the Grove or sometimes to South Miami.*

And smoke a little evil weed, ha! She'd love that.

Family, school, shit, what else? He smiled at himself, of course, jevas. *I go out with a lot of girls. I got some really good lines. Whenever I go out. . .* he remembered the class field trip to the college fair when he got three girls' numbers, *I always come home with at least one telephone number.* Then the phone rang but as soon as he pulled his chair away from the desk, it stopped. The page still wasn't full. He rubbed his hair and drank down the soda. What more, man? Fuck it, whatever. *Right now I got a couple of girlfriends I call all the time. A super cute blonde girl from Miami Springs who's name is Gloria. She's a tremendous dancer. The other girl is not as pretty but super nice and real smart.* More, he bit his lip. *She's Cuban too.* The phone rang again but steadily this time while he scrawled out the last sentences. *I don't like American girls. Their too loose.*

Just as Papo had suspected that morning, baseball practice was suspended because of the rain. He caught a ride with some guys from the team and once home, tipped down a large green tin of soda crackers from atop the refrigerator. When there were only three broken crackers left he replaced the lid and put the container back. There was only enough milk for tomorrow's café so he drank a tall glass of water instead. He watched cartoons on the little black and white set on the kitchen counter with a book and papers in front of him. It was almost five when Matilde,

Manny's mother, got home and the rain had stopped.

"What a way to rain, eh?" she said in Spanish as she put some bags down on the chair next to him.

"Qué pasa, vieja?" he said looking over his shoulder at the large, slightly hunch-backed woman. He arched his long neck up to kiss her. "Manolito's coming home late today."

"Where'd he go?" She pulled some salted codfish from a bag and began to unwrap it while stepping out of her shoes, exposing bright red feet.

Papo gathered his math homework together while he tried to answer absently, "He told me this morning but I forgot."

She shook her head and clicked her tongue and teeth together letting saliva slide through.

"Don't fry me no eggs," he said and they looked at each other and laughed.

Papo left her and the hissing pressure cooker to the now fishy smelling kitchen. He went into his and Manny's room and drew the thick curtain aside to let a bright dirt-speckled sunbeam shine onto the brown carpet. He sighed and pulled out his English assignment to look it over; figured he'd get it out of the way. He looked for a decent pen and when he found one he laid belly-down, his legs spread out wide on the rug with a folder and paper in front of him in the middle of the sunshine.

Begin in the beginning, right, so, that means el campo. *I'm from el campo in Cuba-Remedios, Villa Clara, way in the interior.* Campo, Las Villas, guajiros! He erased el campo and wrote the country instead. *All of my family is guajiro (I don't know the English word for this Miss Fernandez, sorry).* She'll be pissed; he laughed a little. *I lived there until 1980 when I was ten when I came here on a boat.* What a trip! He thought of the first can of soda they were given on the boat that none of them knew how to open. Guess I should tell more about Cuba, shit I spent more than half my life there. *I was very good in school in Cuba.* He remembered his ribbons and certificates. In the third grade he had even gotten the most important one, ah, something, ah, something de la patria. Coño! What was that stupid award?

He shifted his paper to catch more sunlight. He took up the pen again. *I didn't want to leave at first but my mother's family here in Miami gave our names to some people who had a boat.* Stupid assholes, he bit cuticles off his fingertips. He tried to write and bite at the same time but gave up when his handwriting was suffering. *We were...* Shit, how do you say denunciado? Denounced? Yea, that's gotta be it, he wrote *denouced. My mother was thrown out of her job.* Papo bit his right thumb some more as he pictured her losing so much weight and the deep dark circles around her eyes after his father's death and before her own. He pressed down hard on the paper. *The people she worked with hit her and kicked her out.* There was blood on his finger where he had pulled some dead skin off so he stuck it in his mouth and continued. *A group of students ran after my dad with rocks and sticks.* There was a photo of his father stuck in the mirror frame over the dresser. Papo had taken it when his dad was standing next to the big truck before it was totaled. His eyes wandered back to the bottom of the page. Sticks, rocks, oh yea, those bastards. *Some of them kids went to school with me.* He reread the page and when he was done he added a few more lines. *I was spit on which made me very angry but they wouldn't not listen to me. I kept telling them, I want to stay, I don't wanna go. But even my friends called me gusano.* Worm? He asked himself but decided to leave it at that. He turned the paper over and wrote a line on the back before remembering that he wasn't supposed to do that. Coño, he erased the erasable ink and started over on a new sheet.

Even though I didn't want to come here, I got over it all the first time I watched American television. Ah, carajo, that sounds stupid. He erased this and began again. *When I got to this country I learned English right away! I did all right in school but I thought it was boring.* It still is, he turned onto his side and propped up his head. *I had learned most of that stuff in Cuba. For example, the science and math.* He crossed his long legs and chuckled as he continued. *I'm telling you I was very smart in Cuba. I would get "sobresaliente" in all my subjects.* What else can I invent now, he still had more than half way to go. *I have always loved to play baseball.* He thought of his new varsity jacket and added, *I'm a really good pitcher. Coach Manero is pretty good but the team sucks.* Qué más, qué más? *I help him in his Driver's Ed class for an elective credit but I don't do anything in there.* Just sleep.

He got up and went to pee then plopped back down on the floor and took out the last sheet though there were still three lines left on the second page.

It's baseball season so I don't have a girlfriend now. I don't have time, or a car. Should I explain? He sucked some more blood from his finger and yanked another bit of skin from the other side of his fingernail. What the hell. *I live in my best friend's house with his parents. I been with them almost three years now because my father died in an accident.* He wrote very quickly. *My mother died a month after him.* He sat up with his legs stretched out in front of him with the paper in between, thinking. He bounced the backs of his knees on the rug. *My mother's cousins didn't want anything to do with me because they said I was trouble.* Ha, if they only knew that their angel Susanita was doing crack! He shifted his hips again. *I went to live with them for a few months but it was impossible. I hated them almost as much as they hated me.* Shit eaters; he spit out some dead skin. *My mother never really got along with them anyway so I ran away. Manny was my best friend and my mom worked with his mom so they let me stay.* Wonder where that asshole is? *I like his mother alot but sometimes she nags.* He could smell espresso brewing in the kitchen, so he called out to Matilde for a cup. *She's all right. Manolo, the old man, he's hardly around but I like him too.*

He only had a few lines to go when Matilde brought the steaming small cup to him and waited while he gulped.

"Gracias, señora," Papo said coyly, reaching up to pinch her behind when she turned away.

"Niño!" She called out, laughed and left.

Ay, what else can I say? *Manolo works a couple a jobs but me and Manny think he's got a querida.* He read the last sentence aloud then quickly erased it. Damn! Can't do that shit to him, as he recalled one day they were skipping and had seen Manolo's car down near South Beach. He bit what was left of the cuticles on both hands and thought of his part-time. *I work at the Stop-and-Shop on 81st on the weekends. I can't work during the week because of baseball practice.* Papo looked at his mutilated fingers, disgusted, he added one last line, *I'm saving for a car.* But he was still thinking of the old man. Manny and Papo had known that at any minute a woman would step out of the old hotel and get into Manolo's car but neither one of them stuck around to see who she was. Ojos que no ven, corazón que no siente, he sighed out.

Ray dressed hurriedly, jeans first, shoes and shirt last. Ten minutes before, Debbie had sent away her little brother with a couple of dollars to go to the convenience store and get some ice cream. Ray kissed her with one hand cupping the back of her head while she encircled his small waist.

"See ya tomorrow, babe." He was already dashing down the side alley when he heard her say, "Call me tonight."

Ray was distracted in thought on the long walk home. He dug into his tight pockets even though he knew there weren't any cigarettes left. Not enough money for the bus either; should have asked Debbie. Every once in a while he caught wind of the salt air and filled his lungs with it. Around and in front of him large puddles were evaporating in the heat but he wasn't looking down but up at the house numbers along Harding Avenue. He stopped in front of a faded turquoise house with a wide tiled porch. A lean cat was sleeping on a rusted wire chair; it lifted its head at Ray's first steps then bolted across the scraggly grass. Ray opened the screen door and knocked on Dulce María's apartment door to the right.

"Coming," she said in Spanish from inside. He could hear the t.v. from the front room.

"Es René," he said his real name.

"Hey, what happened to you fifth period? You missed the review for the test, dummy." She kissed him on the cheek.

He ruffled her little sister's hair when she looked up to say hello to him. His face was burning and he was starting to smell the sweat from under his arms.

"I went to the park. That old man annoys me." He spoke quietly in Spanish. She sat down in a chair across the room from him, her eyes wrinkled at the corners from smiling.

"I'll give you my notes."

"Naw, that's all right. I'm failing anyway. I gotta go to summer school anyhow." He looked at her clear smooth skin; she didn't have any pimples at all.

"I'm going too. I wanna get all my P.E. credits out of the way." Her eyes were drawn to the t.v. for a moment.

He pushed his soaking back into the sofa before speaking. "I think I'm gonna have to take P.E. too cause Coach Benson can't stand me." He thumbed through his thick-cropped hair. "We can only take two classes right?"

"Yea, think so." She turned up one corner of her mouth while he watched her scratching a mosquito bite on her arm. "How you doing in your other classes?" Her tanned legs were crossed up on the easy chair. Her sister, Ana Lourdes, crawled close by him, poked his ribs and then jumped away. Dulce María slapped her behind as she ran past them into the kitchen laughing.

"So fresh! Wait until I tell Mami," she said.

Dulce's eyes flashed brightly and René could not take it.

He got up and stuck both hands in his front pockets. "I gotta go. You just reminded me about some homework I have for English. I hate that class. She's always making us write."

"What do you expect, René? It's English." She shook her freckled shoulders free of thick locks of hair. "You have to write an essay on your life, right? Magaly told me about it on the way home."

"Yea, some bullshit." He shifted his feet and looked at the t.v.

"You want something to drink?"

"Naw, I gotta go." He looked at her face, so clean. Big soft brown eyes. He could tell that she had washed her hair cause it smelled good and by the way it bounced around. He bit his lip and stepped to the door. "I'll see you tomorrow." He had turned away, touching the cold doorknob when she came over to kiss him on the lips. His knuckles were white from holding the door tight. He gently placed both limp hands on her bare shoulders, inhaling her scent. They stood awkwardly close together for a few seconds before she said, "Hasta mañana, René." It seemed to him that her lips were also shaking.

He took up a quick pace on the way to his building. He tried to remember everything he had said to Dulce María, but it was fruitless, his heart beating so hard in his chest he could hardly concentrate. He mumbled to himself the three blocks over, and repeated fragments of the conversation to the warm sea breeze.

At home, his mother had left a note taped to the shiny metal cabinet over the sink that a Mr. Benson had called about him being absent. Fuck that bastard; Ray crushed the note in his hand and slammed it against the counter, then shook his head, visualizing his report card, a column of F's and then not graduating in time. Qué mierda! Math test tomorrow, Benson'll probably get me internal suspension, oh shit, and the essay.

He found some of his mother's cigarettes in the top drawer. He felt that five minutes had passed when he finished the pack although really an hour had slipped by. The phone's loud ring made him jump a bit in the chair and it sounded like he was out of breath when he answered it.

"You just get there?" His mother's soft voice was all but obscured by the machines in the background.

He coughed a little. "No, no, I been here."

"Why didn't you go to school today?" She spoke even lower so he pushed the receiver closer to his ear.

"I did go. I just didn't go to P.E. I didn't have my shorts and he gives us an F if we don't dress out so why bother?"

"My son, go anyway."

There was a long pause where the sewing machines whirred on and on and he could hear steam blowing from the presses near his mother.

"Renesito, you're a man already, doesn't it embarrass you that teachers call me?"

"Aw, Ma, that guy has it out for me. I should just quit and to hell with it all."

A buzzer sounded; his mother talked to someone next to her before answering him.

"Listen to me, I have to get back but I want you to think about what you just said and remember your mother over here sweating like a pig and putting zippers on jeans." She was quiet another moment. "I don't have to tell you anything more. I'll see you later. There's still some boliche left. Eat."

Her goodbye was drowned out by a second, longer buzzer. After hanging up, Ray rubbed his face in his hands, peeled off the sticky shirt and curled his nose at his strong smelly sweat. A fierce point of pain centered itself between his eyes, making him shut them for another minute while anger whirled around inside his head. It worked its way, trembling, through his muscled shoulders and arms. Hot salty tears burned him but before they could fall, he wiped them away and jammed his chin into his chest to steady the shaking. He drew many heavy breaths and after a great while, he had settled down.

I gotta get my shit together he said to himself as he tried to remember what he was supposed to do for English. He cursed himself for not writing down the assignment and thought about what Dulce María had said. About my life, ay, what a big shit. Ray's eyes moved around and around looking for a spot to focus while the pen in his hand grew heavier and thicker.

When he finally wrote, he wrote without stopping, pressing down so hard that the rest of notebook held the impressions. *What the hell do you wanna know about me anyway?* The first sentence shocked him into moving onto the next. *It's none of your fucking business.* He was sweating and reading as he wrote. *What for? So you can call my mother and bother her with bullshit. She works nights and sleeps days, allright. You wanna talk to her, I'll give her the message.* His hand was cramping but he could not stop now. *You people make me sick. Think you know everything. You don't know shit about me, allright?* His fingers were numb with the last line, which he indented. *Go ahead give me a zero.*

EL LOCO

"YOU MEAN THIS guy hasn't been found competent yet?"

There they are, my doctors—the balding man and my pretty young cubanita—with their clipboards and white smocks.

"What do you want me to do? He's got severe language handicaps, he's illiterate, and has sixty percent hearing loss in both ears."

My back's to the narrow cot and I can't help thinking it's just like in Cuba.

"Jesus, Elena, can't you get anything out of him?"

Well, maybe not; the food's better here. I start to smile then burst out in the hacking laughter I can't hold back which causes the others to move away, slowly at first then quickly out of sight.

"You expect too much from me, Dan."

This morning I went to the fried chicken restaurant next to the Miami River to pick through the table scraps. Some guy with a tie tried to make me leave but because I didn't feel like it, the conflict only ended when the police arrived and threw me out. Always the same shit, always. Now, I'll go back to the bridge and see if that old man has some food I can take. Maybe he won't be there and I can do it without any trouble. These new sneakers are such a relief from the thick tight shoes I got from that big church

by the tracks. I'm so hungry this minute, I'll even eat that stuff from the
cans the old man has. So stupid to give it to those goddamned animals. If
they saw him giving food to cats in Cuba they'd kill him instead of just
killing the cats like I did the other night when the old man wasn't around. I
put them in a sack that I found by the seawall. Just picked ` em up—he's
tamed them so that they can't survive now without him—and tossed them
into the clear green bay. I got away from there with six cans—and a gun.
Damn thing scared the shit outta me when it popped so I dumped it in the
weeds next to the expressway.

"He was held at the hospital in Gainesville in '81. Passive, never
refused treatment; only thing is he couldn't talk right. They just
thought that their Spanish interpreter was bad. He was released
when they needed bed space. Gainesville said they had done
all they could for him. His handwriting is chicken-scratch and
what comes out of his mouth is hardly intelligible. Think he was
shipped back here to a halfway house sometime in 1982. From
then 'til he was picked up by the Miami Beach Police, God only
knows what he's been doing."

"He's been here for a year and a half now and we had to
rule him incompetent in six months or declare him competent
to stand trial. The D.A.'s been on my back because that cop's
family threw a petition at her with 5,000 signatures on it just to
get this moving. I mean, the guy was about to retire, thirty years
on the force, you know, they want to crucify him."

"Dan, I've seen him three or four times already and he's
impossible. I think he lost his hearing as a result of some beating
he got and the speech impairment complicates everything. He's
so weird too. He acts so polite with me and all, but the fourth
floor staff all hate him."

"He's got the hots for you."

"Don't make me ill. He's so disgusting; he smiles at me with those broken teeth and then puts his arms right across the table as if to show me his scars. Please, Dan, can't Sydney see him? I have a stack of files to get to and that conference's coming up."

"Come on, Elena, you're the only true bilingual. Sydney's been bellyaching about his overtime and there haven't been any decent applicants for Javier's job. Give him one more shot and tell me your results by the end of next week. I'm counting on you."

I think I'll go to that house where I was when I first got to Miami. They had tasty food there but that big black man in the kitchen always spat in the soup. Maybe not. Better to go to the bridge. There is a nice slope there next to the water where I can take a nap. It's good to see the people fishing from there. I should try to get some fish but I'd hate to clean it with this puny pocketknife. I had a good one back there. What I would do for fried bonito!

To think that I spent half of my life fishing. Such days on that spar-kling blue sea! Just me and my little boat, my radio. On good days I'd bring in enough for the quota and for me and everyone in the building. Josefina would always give me batter to fry some grunts but there never was enough grease in those days to spare. Sometimes I could pick up the Miami broad-casts. Some snapper, dolphin, once in a while a swordfish. What more could a man want?

They couldn't understand that I had drifted for hours—falling asleep like I did that sunny day. Must have been the wine Julita brought me the night before. Hadn't drunk wine for fifteen years. Even the sunburn didn't bother me. Never felt the anchor line snap. Only the motors from the guard boat woke me.

Half of my life without schooling. What need did I have to write?

Read? From seven years old I fished with my father—he didn't write or read, either. When they came ` round with that blasted committee to teach everyone at night, I only went to see the women. Some pretty young teachers they were. That lovely Julia. What an ass!

It was Julia who pleaded with the officials. For nothing, sweet thing. Already rotting away, the living daylights beat outta me. Didn't realize for days, maybe weeks, how bad. They didn't either but they finally let me alone. Until Mariel.

I tried to see if my boat was nearby when they took me to the port. Never saw so many boats. Racing boats, yachts, barges, big fishing vessels—even in my dreams I couldn't have pictured such a variety. Think a tug boat was there too! I was assigned to a big barge—must have been 300 of us on it. All scared shitless. I was just so happy to see the water again, smell the salt breeze. Didn't get sick once all the way to Key West.

"Let me see number 4-3-7-50-50, Jim."

"Oh, the deadbeat. When you gonna get 'em outta here, Doc? He stinks something awful."

"I don't know. Just wish I could make some progress."

"Well, he is. Every time you leave he jerks off."

"That's lovely, Jim. Thanks."

The first man I killed was a skinny guy with a blue and white hat and matching shirt. He had simply walked down Calle Ocho with a smile that brought my torturer back to life. He looked just like him. So damn skinny, like Gutierrez. I couldn't help it. It was him, to me, it was him. Felt bad after that though, but the poor bastard had such a smile. Even stayed glued to his lips when I pulled the stupid little pocketknife outta his gut. I knew it was all right then; anybody die with a smile like that was ready to go.

That pretty Dr. Montes is coming for me, I know. She has been the only doctor who speaks halfway decent Spanish. Those fucking Cuban guards don't do anything but curse so I curse and spit back at them. I love to see her contort her delicate eyebrows trying to find a way to make me understand. I don't mind lying to her because it always brings her back. It's been a long time this time, but she's back.

"How are you?"

She smiles. What beautiful eyes—green like the bay. I smile back, forgetting my teeth. She frowns a little and looks down at her papers and starts business-like with her questions all over again like every other time. She wants me to tell her if I knew what I did. I always tell her that I was fishing and fell asleep but she can't understand because my tongue is so mangled and I can't distinguish what I say anyway so I could just as well tell her the truth. That that fucking policeman kicked me in the belly and tried to throw me in the dumpster so I took his gun and made him stop. He thought I was drunk; he provoked me. Son of a whore got what he was looking for.

"Is this your real name?" Her shiny pale lips move. She points to a neatly printed assortment of letters. I take the pen from her tanned hands; her nails are painted pink with thin white moon slivers over the tips of them. She pulled away a little at first until I began to write on the blank pad. I signed my name—José Manuel Escobar Vidal. I know she has a hard time reading my script, so I write this very carefully. She nods at it and makes a little check on her paper.

"Do you know where you are?" She asks and writes it down for me. I tap on the table, take the pen and write "USA" for her. She seems to think this is good so she keeps asking and today I answer—stupid things I never did before. How old I am; where was I before coming here; do I have any family. Harmless things like that. Her perfume is sweet; I take her pen to sniff it. Must be some gardenia in it.

The second man I killed was about to kill me. He did not look like my wardens. It was a young man, maybe a boy, I don't know, a very tall Gringo. Blonde and heavy with square-tipped brown boots. He had a two by four and I had seen him cracking some other guy's skull open the week before by the big park downtown. He thought I was asleep but only drunks sleep at night. When he raised it high over his head I kicked him in the balls with my thick, tight shoes. The board fell down the embankment. I scrambled toward it and gave it back to him—right by his temple. Lucky for me that knocked him out. He was a big one! Took me a while to pull him to the water and roll him in, board and all. Really wanted those boots though. They wouldn't budge. There were some bums watching from the other side of the bridge but they laughed and waved at me. I lit outta there right after.

"Do you know who this is?" She shows me a picture of that fat grey-haired cop. I forget to not smile so she's writing stuff on her paper and I write, very carefully this time, that he is policía gordo. She smiles too but I guess she remembers she's not supposed to so she twists her fine features into line again. I've had her all to myself for over an hour today. How she shifts her hips in that seat!

"Why did you shoot him?" She's very serious now and looks at my face while she puts the paper in front of me. I love the sad look she has and I decide I will do anything to make her keep looking at me like that. I write for about five minutes. She struggles to read my poor writing upside down but at last I give it to her and now I can watch her read. She has long curly light brown hair which streams over her small shoulders. Sometimes she brushes it away and crosses and re-crosses her legs underneath. What legs—she'd put Julia to shame. This woman is very elegant. Just look at those hands and such smooth skin. I love the way she turns the paper sideways to write—left-handed like me. I intend on cooperating today to make her stay here.

When she's finished reading, she moves the paper back to me and points to some words. I rewrite them for her as she watches me. I hurry because I want to look, not be looked at.

"Is this correct?" She has rewritten it completely and puts it before me so I have to read. It says:

> The fat policeman hitting, kicking me.
> I defended myself. He push me into
> garbage, beating me all the time.
> Self-defense. He did it before.
> Sleeping at the beach one day under
> the pier and he got me with bigclub
> they all have. He provoked me, doctor.

I began to rush through it but the handwriting was so even and fine that I wanted to lick every single letter, eat every last word. She was watching me but I was looking at her sentences so I took my time. When I had enough, I told her that it was the truth. She nodded and asked if I was sure. I nodded back and couldn't keep from smiling at those light green eyes.

- A -

I don't want to let her leave me this time so I grab her arm with its silky flesh as she starts to get up. She's afraid and calls out and that asshole guard rushes in. I've had it with him once and for all so I try to take out my little knife except I forget it's not there and he shoots. Three times I think. I'm not sure because I'm thinking of the blue-green sea and Dr. Montes' wide, round eyes.

- B -

"Elena, what are you doing to me? El Loco competent? Come on, self-defense? Damn it, I thought you said he couldn't talk."

"Wouldn't talk, Dan. Talked plenty last week. Actually he wrote down exactly what happened. I confirmed it. Get someone else to concur—gotta be bilingual."

"Stan's going on vacation next week, so I'll have to get an outsider. Shit! The D.A.'ll love this. Can you imagine the trial? One person to decode his writing, another to translate for the judge and jury, it'll be a circus."

"And for what? They're gonna fry 'em away. I saw the cop's family on t.v. the other night. They want this guy's ass bad. Such bullshit."

"Did you do anything different when you interviewed him this time?"

"No, not really. He just cooperated. I mean he really answered the questions. Other times he'd scribble or slur in that incoherent way he does without paying attention to the questions. What could I say? 'Gee, Mr. El Loco, why are you cooperating?'"

"I just don't get it. This'll never end now."

- C -

It's been two weeks since my doctor has come to see me. I really hope she gets here soon ` cause these guards are really bothering me. Yesterday they *wouldn't let me alone. Made me leave the big room when I was so caught up in thoughts of her. Wasn't even done.*

There's someone coming now. Wish it's her—though I'm in a bad way today.

It's not, damn it! Some fucking big-nosed bastard instead. I don't want him so when he sets his papers and pads in front of me I sweep them off the desk. He gets up, I start yelling and the guards come and push me around but the tall black one pushes a stick in between my ribs so I bite him. After they hit me for a while and pin me down I see her through the window in the door. She looks so worried, poor angel, then I blank out.

MUCHACHA (AFTER JAMAICA)

WASH YOUR PANTIES and stockings when you take them off; always carry a perfumed handkerchief in your bosom; fry *frituritas de bacalao* in shimmering hot oil; ask for a little extra when you buy cloth from the *polacos*; wearing those pointed shoes will cripple you!; don't let me catch you talking to those boys hanging out on a corner by the empty lot; **but I don't talk to 'em**; you mustn't refer to papaya as papaya but as *fruta bomba* because people might think you're indecent; it's all right to call those little rolls *bollitos* though; **now that's nasty**; this is the way you embroider a woman's hankie; this is the way you embroider a man's; this is the way you mend a sock; this is the way you iron a *guayabera* without messing up the pleats; this is the way you starch your fine linen blouses that you embroider; this is the way to take *la grasa* out of the soup; this is the way you sort the frijoles; this is the way you wash the rice; **but *madrina* doesn't wash the rice**; plant the cilantro under the kitchen window so you know when it's ready; these are the herbs and spices for *el lechoncito*, remember to use sour oranges' juice for the *mojo* on *noche buena*; this is how you grind the herbs and spices; don't throw the *fruta bomba* seeds near the house they grow *silvestre*; this *silvestre* is used to calm the nerves; this leaf is cut in the middle and spread on burns to prevent scars, it can be drunk too for the lungs but watercress is the best for the lungs; this one is to ease your cramps; this is how you wash the porch; always soak bloodstains in icy cold water; **they still won't come out**; don't keep any stained clothing; wrap red rags around your fruit trees to ward off the evil eye; always wear your *azabache* for the same reason, I will give one to your firstborn; never play music on *viernes santo*; don't ever let me catch you cursing; **but you and . . .** ; don't sit with your legs open, it's indecent and you're a decent girl; wash your chocha with that peach tin can from under the sink, always; don't eat at anybody's house; don't give your picture to anyone; do not put your fingers with *merengue* in the pig's mouth, can't you see that animal has teeth?; don't dance the *merengue* too close; don't let any man stand behind you on the bus; show your husband everything but your *culo*, you can never show a man everything; this is how you make flan; this is how to *despojarte* with branches of the *paraíso*; this is how you float the gardenias so they don't turn brown, plant them under the bedroom window when they take root so they perfume your nights; don't eat all the *anónes,* other people like them too; this is how you embrace your child; this is how you embrace someone else's child; I don't have to tell you how to embrace your husband; this is how you embrace other women; always *saluda* when you walk in anywhere, you're not just anyone, you know; don't wear black bras, you'll look like the *fletera* from across the street; always use the formal *usted* when speaking to people you don't know; don't throw dishes at each other when you fight; don't let your inlaws meddle in your matrimony, that doesn't include me; don't talk Spanish at the factory/school/office; don't throw the house out the window; don't drive the oxcart in front of the oxen; don't make fun of *guajiros*, your father will be hurt; don't make fun of *gallegos*, your grandmother will be hurt; this is how you take a bath without running water; this is how to make a *cortadito*; this is how you save your pennies; this is how you keep your shoes in good condition; you mustn't let the full moon shine on you when you're sleeping; when you call someone on the telephone always say *buenos días* or *buenas tardes*, you have manners, you know; this is how you make *camarones enchilados*; this is how you avoid being used, if it happens, it's your own fault and don't let it happen again; this is where you place the glasses full of water for the saints; this is where you put their food; this is how you light a candle for the dead; this is how you pray for the living; this is how you will mourn your *tierra*; **but this is my country**; this is how you will live in exile; this is how your spirit will rise when your body falls but only after many years, *mi hijita*, so don't worry about that now.

FAILED SECRETS

THERE IS NO one to whom you can tell this story, abuelita; it is sealed tight, cauterized with thick keloid skin, smooth and impenetrable. So, I tell it, filling in all the blanks. Going back to the brief, blessed time when love, trust and safety is the kind embrace of a doting father, your protector. But he dies when you are seven, your padre, your saint. And she—beautiful, distracted, who enjoys the company of men more than motherhood—offers no comfort. She remarries quickly. Is this when you learn to fight?

The potent male likes you, little stick-skinny girl with expressive eyes and vulnerable lips. He makes love to your mother and fucks you. Was it one of her lovers or a stepfather who violated your core, shattering your belief in love? Did she accuse you of baiting him?

You get skinnier and there's a campaign initiated to fatten you up; a different type of bean every day, meat run through the grinder, thinner than the air surrounding you. At one point, you are forced to drink fresh calf's blood to fortify your own, your deep-socketed eyes and jutting cheekbones incriminates them. Then your baby sister's born colicky, just in time. You can go off to school, and mother doesn't care that your socks are

falling around your ankles and your shoes aren't brightly polished. She's just glad you are out of the house so she can put that
child down and sleep (you carry the baby every chance you get,
soothing her with old songs you remember from papi; it doesn't
help though it calms you).

You excel in school, higher scores every year; you even win
a prize for recitation of a patriot's nationalist lyric. Some popular girls adopt you, their skinny but almost pretty friend. Many
of them plan purposeful lives, university studies. It is 1943; in
Cuba women now can be professionals—besides teachers. You
dream of being a doctor. It makes sense. Your grandfather stud-
ied medicine (until he was disowned by his family for slumming
with la puta negra—dark hussy); your father tried to become a
pharmacist. You decide to ask for your patrimony; grandfather
left money, properties.

One day after school, you approach your mother, who is sitting on the wide front porch in the afternoon breeze.

*I want to have my share. I want to go to university, to study medi-
cine.*

Did she laugh? Did she pause before she crushed your dream
to bits under her stacked heel? Did she turn to her lover and
comment on the wastefulness of educating girls?

Was this betrayal worse than the first?

You decide to get away; it takes some doing—girls don't
leave the house unless they're married. But by then another
baby sister and your oldest sister's children crowd the house.
Nineteen, unmarried, you go to live with the eccentric maiden
aunt. After all, everyone expects you to follow suit. You work
in your father's family's pharmacy, mixing tonics, giving injec-
tions. You are in heaven all day, until evening when you return to

113

a bare room, bed bug-ridden mattress, peephole reopened every night by the neighbor pervert. In a nightmare, you see yourself tubercular, like your aunt coughing in the next room, living in squalor even while there is means to avoid it, you almost understand the pride and think you can learn to embrace it but in the morning you awake to blood-covered sheets and oozing scabs all over.

You decide to get away again, this time to leave completely. The first leaving was easy, just across the city and without scandal. This time you take a plane to live with a school chum who's gone to el norte. She lives in a boarding house run by a Spanish matron who has seven sons who need wives—willing to marry them off to Cuban sluts since they are neither handsome nor skilled. You are twenty-two, undereducated but not ignorant, single, speak no English, and have never been anywhere outside of Havana but your passport is a door you intend to step through without ever looking back. The plane lands in Miami; you board a bus to New Jersey and hope to God Alma will be there when you arrive. She is and you are finally safe, arrived in this new life.

This fight might be difficult at times, your tongue thickens at every attempt in the new brutish language, but it is easier than being back on the island. You get by, taking shitty jobs in factories surrounded by unintelligible Polish and Italian ladies sewing dainties for years, but every night you go to the movies and listen over and over to the dialogue, deciphering the romance of America. And every night you can go to your own apartment, not a home but your own room and sleep in a clean bed with clean sheets. No peeping toms and no immediate danger.

You order your own life without regard to what others

think—those others are left far behind, across the ocean. No one sees what you do or don't do. If you take English classes at night, go to church everyday, no one will ridicule you. You are expert at economizing, save all your pennies but things are difficult in Cuba and you start to send money, generously acknowledged by your sisters. You feel guilty, not knowing exactly why but you learn to accept your independence. You learn to be proud of your strength built on such a scrawny frame that shakes sometimes, knocking your no-longer skinny knees together.

You didn't have to tell me your secrets, you see. They betrayed themselves over the years anyway. But tell me, abuelita, what did I miss?

PuYAS

[puya: a steel point; the spur of a rooster; a hint]

"A LAS OCHO estuviera en la clase de química." Lidia had looked up and around and spoken to all the hundreds of others like her, dazed, hungry, sun burnt, exiled. The others, like her, could not find any particular face to focus on, so they looked around and around them, missing each other. She was fifteen back then in 1980, and at eight a.m. would have been, if she were still in Cuba, in chemistry class, but she was in Key West, at least her mind was, in an aircraft hanger being processed by haggard, barely bilingual immigration workers. Sometimes, on days when her eyes glaze over the empty face of a clock, Lidia still sees the hanger, the officials, the blank eyes. For Lidia, as for all those others, not just the hundreds but the thousands, the years after the boatlift have been crowded, busy, difficult.

On one of those days when she has found the feeling that places her there, the image of herself that May morning in Key West is conjured up easily. The white cat clock with the swinging rhinestone tail that she faced had smooth shiny cheeks, fat feline features that stare at her. It is in her father's house, in his compañera's kitchen, the same place Lidia had decided that morning she must leave. She said to herself and to her infant son, Jonathan, but not looking at him, "A esta hora estuviera en la clase de química." Yet she knew it wasn't true because by now she would have been a chemical engineer if she had stayed in Cuba, though what she really wanted was to manipulate matter in the way that structural engineers did.

Lidia felt her face arrange itself in that familiar set, the one built to withstand more than plastic clocks. This one's the one that holds up to the now rampant steely looks. The mask is successful because it avoids the angry pointed looks; in it Lidia's eyes become dazed, her vision flounders for something to focus on. That day's mask is the result of a restless night, for who could sleep after the ruckus Madeline raised, isn't that right, papito? But the instant she looked at her son, her facade evaporated. Her father, Ignacio, had no choice really but to side with her, his wife; after all, Lidia was a woman already—in this country at eighteen you are an adult, she recalled.

The three years the three of them had lived together were marked by an ever-increasing tension and pettiness that drove Madeline, Ignacio and Lidia to poisoning bitterness, which gave way to contempt. Madeline picked on Lidia. Lidia ignored Madeline. Ignacio neglected both of them or one of them alternately. When Lidia took Raúl as a lover, he became the reason for their fights. Silence, looming and persistent, sat in and over the house for most of the time she was expecting. It was broken only by the joy of the child's light, but even this changed when Lidia continued to see Raúl so, at last, there was disrespect and this, burning in her mind now because of last night. Daughter of a whore he had dared to call her, daughter of a mother who was dead, who could not defend herself, was what made Lidia decide. Ignacio would never force her out, of course, so she had gathered the few things she had worth carrying and walked away. The tenderness he lavished on his grandson would be something, she knew, they all would miss but staying with them was just too much.

For the last seven months she had been living in a narrow one bedroom apartment that was part of the triplex where Carmen, the woman who took care of Jonathan, lived. Lidia had left her job cutting patterns at the factory where Ignacio pressed pleats. It was hard finding another job that would pay more than minimum wage at first, because such work was plentiful in that city glutted with the undocumented and because the earlier exiles had cut off their original tide of generosity and openess and replaced it with waves of paralyzing hardness. But Lidia managed to get work at a busy Cuban restaurant. Being a young woman and having shapely hips that were attractive to Latins (but much too wide for Anglos) had made it somewhat easier; with the tips of a good week, Lidia took home about thirty dollars more than her factory earnings.

Today, five years after Mariel, she was in her own kitchen and although she had a fleeting thought about engineering when she glanced up to see the time, Lidia's mind was more occupied with the ragged curve of Raúl's beard as he swished coffee about in a demitasse cup. She pulled her long wavy hair away from her now composed face and roped it into a dangling loose knot. His lover for over two years, she had no notions of marriage or living together. Other than their harried pre-dawn mornings in the bedroom where their son also slept, Lidia did not need to own him. And despite their fierce lovemaking—for they were like cats in heat, him biting the back of her neck and she pressing her nails into the tufts of hair on his shoulders and crying out sometimes because no one told her these things were not nice—it was taken for granted that they would live separately, as though the fact that Raúl had never divorced his wife in Cuba meant something. It was just a matter of fact, just as it was a matter of record that his name was left off the birth certificate at the hospital; welfare was more important than family standing. He was only seven years older than her twenty but looked middle-aged. When Lidia would yank out long grey hairs from his scalp and call him viejo, she had only to look at his dry brown arms and face to remind herself of how much the Miami sun had aged him. She thought a moment about her father's drawn face. Maybe it was just Miami.

Lidia sensed Raúl's narrow jaw to be sharper today; his field of vision avoided alighting on his son. She delicately clawed at the tabletop, feeling the cool Formica on her fingertips, waiting for an answer to that angle, while he took one short sip then gulped down the rest of the café. He chased it with a sweating glass of water, slamming it down, startling them. Jonathan began to bubble spit on his pink and white lamb bib. Lidia took away the cup with the broken handle and rinsed the glass. From over Raúl's shoulder, she noticed the hands that would not be still, leathery fingers pulling through stringy strands of flat brown hair. She stood there watching as he stroked his bristled cheek. Finally, when he remembered that Lidia was standing, Raúl gestured for her to sit and took her hands in his.

"Mi vida, last night I spoke with my cousin."

Lidia bit her lip and pointed her chin at him. His voice was hard today too, devoid of the affectionate tone she hoped their son would inherit. She said to herself, Ah yes, Nueva York, the land of milk and honey where you kick up dollar bills with the point of your shoe.

"He is doing very well in the North. He has a big apartment—three bedrooms. And a car. He said he could get me a job that guarantees eight dollars an hour. Eight dollars, Lidi!"

Squeezing her eyelids together before opening them wide, Lidia resisted an inappropriate urge to yawn broadly, which would expose all her bad back teeth. She gritted them instead.

"Pepe says I can live with him free. He really wants me to go try it up there." A blue jay landed noisily on the aluminum awning outside before its own scratching sounds frightened it away.

"And you? Is this what you want?" She forced the words up through her knotted throat but looked away at the baby banging his fists on the playpen's thin mattress.

"I want to try it. At least, give it a chance. Many people have gone there and done well. They pay good in New Jersey." He looked out the small window a moment, trying to follow the jay's cry. Then he turned back to her. "Too many of us here in Miami. I think el norte has to be better than this."

In the corner of her mind, Lidia saw his lonely figure, plastic bags of fruit upraised in both hands, pacing up and down the busy intersection near the dog track. The mamonsillos had attracted her at first. She hadn't eaten those sour green fruit balls since she was a kid when she saw him walking toward her with a bag stuffed full of them. She thrust both arms out of her father's car window almost upsetting them and some small yellow mangoes all over 57th Avenue. He had laughed, joked, eased her father's anger; her father talked about the huge mamonsillos borne by the tree at his mother's finca in Camagüey.

"Poor girl, she thought she'd never see these again. You can't blame her, sir. I went crazy when I first saw them, too."

Lidia's father grudgingly gave up two dollars for her extravagant taste and grabbed a couple himself. She immediately went to work compiling a heap of mamonsillo peels and pits between her legs. Ignacio and Raúl became acquainted, used to each other's existence, at least for a while. She looked forward to seeing him every afternoon coming home from the factory. He'd always have a little bag of fruit for her, then came his visits to the house, afterwards came the trouble.

Her mind shifted back to his blistered feet, his dark deeply wrinkled neck, the fixed blank smile—what Raúl had built to withstand the look. Then it materialized before her embodied in another one of her people's faces. Raúl, Jonathan, the present moment were all lost to that look. She knew that even his deftly constructed grin had become shaken by the looks, for there were many versions of the look, of the drivers he saw as he walked up and down, always in those new and big American cars, down and up the grassy median. Tight features, a piercing stare, the disgust registered in the creases and furrowed brows of the faces of the beholders. Like spikes in the sand, oblique grey arrows out of the warm softness of land and sea, the looks could be buried superficially. Unsuspecting, Lidia could walk into a store on Flagler, people could be talking, gossiping, the city commission, the cocaine cowboys, but most likely it would be about Marielitos. They would stop, elbow each other, then look right at her, totally oblivious of her. Some of them might avert their gazes but she could feel their eyes feeling her when she went down the aisle to get sweet ham from the butcher in the back. One could step into anything on the beach, broken bottles, driftwood, man-of-war jellyfish, remnants of shipwrecks. Some of it may corrode and become barnacle-encrusted, like the iron rods used to fortify long lost piers, but it lies there just beneath the wet sand, waiting for the unprotected foot. Those pointed looks made her remember revolutionary training; her finger itched for a machine gun trigger. Then Lidia herself became hardened; her skin stretched itself taut over a freshly set jaw. Raúl could go to the North and blend in with the Portorros and Dominicanos but Lidia had to fight the look in the enemy's camp. What choice did she have after all? There was no familia to go to, so what was left was to be subversive. Tearing away the mask that inhibited her true face, bit by bit she would erase it, become salt and wind to erode the look from the enemy that was her own people.

Two clenched fists refocused before her. Jonathan had fallen asleep, and Raúl was looking out the window to where the birds were singing, saying he was going to get going.

"When will you be leaving for there?" she asked, his light blue eyes back on her. The child had them too, a blue as warm and clear as the sea off Santa María del Mar where she was born. Lidia wondered whether the ocean up there was blue, what the sand was like. Something to remind one of home.

"Pretty soon. Pepe's leaving Elizabeth tomorrow. Driving straight through. I figure, probably, we'll be starting off Sunday morning. Early." He reached into his pocket and pulled out a wad of singles, fives and tens. "I want you to take this."

"It isn't necessary. You'll need it." She covered his hand with her own. "You helped me out enough with the security deposit here."

"Do me the favor of taking it, Lidi. The least I could do. There is $200."

She thought of the luxuries the money could buy—comfortable shoes, some new panties and a badly needed bra, a toy or two—though the playpen and floor were strewn with once discarded now disinfected toys, she had never actually purchased a toy for Jonathan. But then there were the necessities—medicine, disposable diapers, bus money.

"All right then. I'll put it to good use." She uncrossed her legs; her knees edging toward him.

"I know you will, Lidi." He bit his thin lower lip; a subdued sigh escaped him. "I will miss you."

He touched the side of her face then rested his hand on her shoulder. They got up together. She was still humid from that morning's lovemaking. She tugged at her skirt's loose waistband. Raúl gave her Pepe's phone number written on a piece of torn newspaper. "In case you need anything."

Well, Lidia sighed to herself, she'd get more sleep now that he would not be tapping on her window at five in the morning. It was bound to happen one way or another, she said to herself, watching his small frame walk through the sunny yard, then the gate. He left without seeing, a last time, Jonathan's eyes that were his own.

Lidia found many spaces of time during the days to consider her situation—at the restaurant waiting for her customers' meals to come through the opening from the kitchen where trays of dishes crashed and clattered every few minutes; or that quiet chunk of an hour in the afternoon just before her shift finished when most people came in for a shot of café. On the bus bench, watching the street corner vendors, she wondered whether or not she would see Raúl again, if he had it better up there, if she would ever go up there. This time Lidia was in her apartment squeezing liquid vitamin from a dropper into her son's mouth, starting the morning routine, so mechanical, the child cooperating for once, swallowing the sweet-tasting liquid. Now she was going over the alternative to leaving her father. What a choice. Ay, mamá!

She startled herself again with the now frequent thoughts of her mother. Her singing mother had died when she was twelve and the only child. (Lidia left only a few distant and indifferent cousins in Cuba, an uncle who had broken relations with her mother because of her father and very aged, even then, paternal grandparents.) Her singing mother, Olga Valdés, an orphan with a rasping speaking voice. Neighbors had been as compassionate as could have been expected; they had probably supposed that Lidia really had her grandparents, no one's fault.

The years in Cuba following her mother's death passed so quickly, a blurred space dotted and accented with scholastic and civic certificates. Lidia had dedicated herself in a flurry of activity for the Youth Brigade. When she was fourteen, her father had been caught with a crate of black market vegetables in the trunk of his government car. His taxi permit had been revoked and she had been warned by that "they" of an amorphous body of teachers, counselors, friends, but he was all to her then. Everything, though they lived apart; she in school, he with her grandparents. She rose in his defense. They told her to be careful. He was watched. She was badgered to watch him also. They became suspicious of her. He was transferred to the highway division of the Transportation Ministry. That spring she was studying furiously for her exams at the Upper Preparatory; her honors and loyalty to the Communist Youth facilitated an invitation to join the Party, but they suggested that she renounce her father who had been implicated in an escape scheme and was being questioned. Lidia hadn't spoken to him in weeks, but he was the only one she had. She didn't need to decide because he was released in time for the storming of the Peruvian Embassy gates. He jumped over the wall with Madeline, the woman who was living with him. Lidia anxiously listened to the radio broadcasts from the interior. When Fidel gave the embassy crashers safe-conduct passes to their homes to wait for exile, Lidia was back in Havana. Her father so reduced in size; he and Madeline looked empty. The cuffs of their pants soaked with excrement and urine, their skin and hair stiff with grime. She embraced them; the three of them swaying, her translucent-skinned grandparents crying in each other's thin arms. She stayed with them, leaving the prepa, the grants, the Party, the island.

But now she was looking up, in her own kitchen, squinting her eyes for strains of a song. Lidia's clearest memories of her mother, the sweet low singing, had once been obscured by the years following her death. By school and Brigade drills, fields of yuca, exams and her father, but now he was out of her life; he was not the only one. As a child, Lidia could hear her mother's songs no matter what room she was in. She seemed to create light with her voice for Lidia could not recall a single instant or image of her mother singing and the picture being dim. On her sick bed, she sang, though the cancer had consumed the higher tones and eventually swallowed all the light for itself. Sometimes Lidia felt her mother in the room with her, watching the baby with her, and though she tried to sing herself, she always ended by remaining silent, listening to her saved-up memories instead.

This morning it was her father calling her mother a whore that spoke through her thoughts, though she hummed and tightly shut her lids to find the songs, little décimas, learned from the guajira who raised her mother and who made a guitar sing. His angry words and Madeline's sobs clouded around her, choking the melodies. She had made the right decision, she said to herself. What was that refrán? Mejor sola que mal acompañada; much better off alone than in bad company. She would not have to listen to their running commentary on her life. There would be no more indirectas or puyitas—the hints she so detested, if she could help it. This way was the best way. This way she could concentrate on herself and on her son.

"You know, Americano, we have to get going." Lidia raised Jonathan out of the playpen and high over her head then down into her face. She lightly mouthed his nose then nibbled on his chin. She was looking for more teeth to come in since Carmen had warned her, "They itch him already. That's why his sleep is such a fitful one, his little arms and legs jumping and twitching, always. Little angel, it pains me to see him sleeping so bad."

She rubbed some ointment onto his gums. "You'll probably have to have frenitos, poor thing. Your papá's teeth all stick out and mine's aren't so beautiful either." He gurgled back.

"We'll be all right." She picked up toys around him, gathering his favorites to take to Carmen's. Lidia paused before the mirror in the bathroom to dab on face powder from a compact held together with a rubber band. She poured some of the baby's Royal Violet cologne on her throat and wrists and wiped her hands wet with perfume on his hair. He gurgled some more.

"Today I start the part-time with the arquitectos. Wish me luck, papito." Jonathan screeched happily as she swung their respective bags on one shoulder and scooped him up with her free arm, then lumbered out and around the building, the morning, like most Miami mornings, already bright and warm with sun. "Doña Carmen, es Lidia," she called through the screened and wrought iron door. She could hear her turning down the Radio-Reloj station before coming to let her in. She kissed the older woman on her perspired cheek.

"Oh, so hot, so early." Tiny beads collected on the flared ends of Carmen's nose. "I was just rinsing some things in the sink. Have you found out what bus takes you closest to your new job?" She motioned for Lidia to hand her the baby. "My little love, who gave you that precious hat?" The older woman wiped her face before kissing him on both cheeks. "A miniature man! Hemm. And one that smells so good too."

"My dad got that hat for him on the day he was born. Isn't it true, papito?" She smiled close to his face. "It's only now that it fits him."

After giving birth, before she could return to the clothes factory, Lidia had to find someone who would take care of Jonathan as if he was her own. She had sensed from their first meeting at la clínica that Carmen's wonderful gaze at the child was genuine and she knew instinctively she could trust the woman with the sweet brown skin and loving yellow eyes free of steel. Her look was devoid of scorn; she seemed to really know what it was like for Lidia without being a Marielita herself.

She and Carmen had spent close to two hours in the crowded, noisy waiting room talking. Lidia admired the woman's calm even bearing, her readiness and ease in holding the child, something she herself had not mastered. She asked many questions of the woman about caring for Jonathan, the same questions she had posed to the pediatrician but preferring, trusting, Carmen's answers instead. When Lidia mentioned that she needed someone to take care of him during the days, Carmen immediately offered herself: "I was watching two bigger ones half days but now their mother is putting them in a pre-kinder nursery, is that what they call it?"

Not long after, she had left her father's house and Carmen was delighted to have them both near her, neighbors now, for she lived on the other side of the triplex, sandwiching the landlord's large three-bedroom apartment between them.

"The bus runs every fifteen minutes and I can take it on 27th Avenue." Lidia placed the baby's bag on Carmen's kitchen chair.

"That means you can expect to be waiting on it for about an hour. Twenty-seventh Avenue is almost ten blocks, no?"

"Unfortunately, yes, but I promise to wear a hat." Lidia winked. An unmuffled car roared nearby causing the baby's eyes and mouth to search the air for it.

The large woman smiled and shook her head at the smaller, light-skinned Lidia. "I don't go out in that terrible sun unless I have my umbrella, dear. You have to hide from it; it's enough to crack rocks most days."

"You're right, of course. I don't like to take el niño out in the middle of the day for that same reason." She lifted his hat to smooth back a few fine strands of hair from Jonathan's forehead. "We make our excursions early in the morning, don't we?" She had made it a habit to take him out on her days off after his first bottle, before garbage collections. A favorite spot was the Goodwill drop-off in the little shopping center a few bocks away on Flagler Street. Lidia always dressed him in the most faded of his faded clothes so that if there were any street people rummaging around they would leave her alone though most times they'd actually help find things for him. How much the Americans threw away! The clothes she found could have sold for dear amounts in Cuba, they were in such good condition. She had even picked up a toaster-oven—all she could gather from examining it was that the previous owner was probably distracted by the chipped plastic knob in front. Other treasured finds included a scorched iron that came clean with some steel wool and an intact set of stoneware plates.

"I made some malanga for us," Lidia said, pulling out a covered plastic bowl and placing it on the narrow counter. "Try and see if he'll take it."

"Claro, I'm glad to hear it. The child should be eating table food. Nothing like some viandas for a baby. A little strained cassava and carrots, boniato, plátano." She pushed his cheeks together to pout his lips. "And now that this little man has a tooth!"

Lidia left them babbling to each other. She started out walking briskly toward the bus stop despite the June heat, though she lingered near the tall orchid trees bordering the broad avenue. Trampled blossoms were embedded in the evenly grooved pavement. There was no one around—too early for those lookers with points in their eyes. She pulled one of the lavender flowers off a low limb and raised it to her nostrils. How can such a pretty thing not smell, she thought, then tossed it down among the others just falling.

When she reported to work that afternoon at 4:00, after the eight-hour shift at the restaurant, Lidia could not help but feel giddy from enthusiasm. At the interview, Silva had nodded, praised the sketches she'd done for him, right on the spot, even with him looking at her, his eyes clothed with tinted glasses.

"Not bad. I'll give you a chance. Where did you learn to draw? Obviously, it's a temporary position; we have so much work now. I've had to hire a full timer too. Probably six months." But Lidia was undaunted; she was to work behind broad tilted drafting tables—maybe one of her own. There would be shiny extension lamps to move to different angles, scores of pencils, pens, markers and paints in every conceivable color, and thick and thin brushes made of the softest hair and pad after pad of huge sheets of paper. Blank or lined, white or green, there would be much paper to fill, even if only for six months.

She had rushed home to shower and change and check in on Carmen and el niño before catching the bus to the Miracle Mile architect's office. To Lidia, it was a space-age wonder, though she pondered a glass block wall and the many low circling ceiling fans, trying to fit them in with the modern interior and the centrally air-conditioned office. Sleek drawings displayed along the walls stirred Lidia's thoughts back to school age dreams, the hopes she had had for the committee to let her change her course of study from chemical engineering to structural engineering; but by the time she was fifteen, she had excelled in organic and inorganic chemistry and mastered all the algebra, trig and calculus courses at the grant school in the country. Although her young mind had raced with formulas, experiments and solutions, in her heart she hungered for iron, concrete and cables. She wanted to plan buildings, to draw those x-ray vision images that held together tons of material that held up tons of people. Well, drafting is a start anyway, she said to herself, pushing through the polished aluminum door. A receptionist looked up from the tinkling of chimes over Lidia at the entrance.

"Can I help you in something?" She smiled broadly through

bright pink-colored lips framing wired teeth.

"My name is Lidia Cruz. I've come to . . ." She was cut off by snapping metal gums spewing English.

"Oh, yeah. Through that door. Toni's, eh, Mr. Silva's in the back." She lowered her mascara-thick lashes to a fashion magazine before her.

"Ahí." Lidia slowly stepped toward the door though her heart pounded. "El ingeniero Silva me espera?"

The younger woman did not look up but pointed with a long square lacquered nail. "In there."

Another polished door but this one, though it appeared heavy and too cumbersome to move, swished smoothly and efficiently along the silvery blue carpet.

A voice came from the back of the large bright room. "Señorita Cruz, cómo estás?" Silva looked up briefly then turned his eyes back to the large plan before him and the head draftsman standing next to him. There were a couple of men at some tables to the left and right who were putting their things away. They turned to watch her walk down the aisle while she concentrated on Silva, who was calculating some figures on a zipping and popping calculator. She could feel the men's eyes at her back, but these were safe though, just male looks focusing on her hips held firm in the straight white skirt. The draftsman at the boss's side also glanced up to eye her but turned away when she met his gaze inching its way up her torso.

"Un momentico, eh, niña?" Silva lifted a thick hand; the nails were filed and buffed.

So, Lidia thought, this is how it will be. She bit her lip and tasted the sweet cheap lip-gloss. Her fingers itched this time for the sharpened pencils.

She was very good at her drafting job. Sharp, clean drawings. Poignant, efficient lines. Her sketches earned her tolerance from the others, all men, whose looks had evolved, not diminished. They were masked by piropos, but their flattery was always suspect, never simply motivated by sexual greed but by what Lidia knew was rooted in her label; in what Raúl fled from, yet which flew in his face up north and everywhere. Her co-workers, exiles themselves, from her own island, or from other islands and lands where Spanish bonded them into one people and yet, those circumstances could not disguise what was beneath the admiring glances. As a woman, an exile, a co-worker, even though she was attracted to one or more of them and her breasts and hips were beside themselves for lovers, Lidia fought them. Their provoking looks, with those points lodged just behind the corneas, somewhere between the irises and the pupils, did not fool her; though she fought herself, told herself: you can use *them*. It can be convenient. But the arrangement with Raúl was nothing of the sort, she answered herself back. So she slept with herself or with Raúl whenever he was in town and she drank the bitter tea, inserted the soaked sponge Carmen gave her. Many months shifted by and the looks corroded. The looks, the ones earlier émigrés once saved for Marielitos like herself were still present, but Lidia perceived them to be worn out and tired as time walked on.

Now when she went to the market Lidia drove the car there, the one her father sold her for $400. He was back in her life, visiting, occasionally arriving with Madeline, bringing Jonathan gifts of plastic robots and guns. Now when Lidia went to pay for the sweet ham and Cuban crackers, the cashier was most likely a Marielita like herself, smiling, chatty—that new Nicaraguan restaurant down the street, the first Cuban-born candidate running for mayor, oh, and are you taking your kids to the Youth Fair, too?

Lidia continued taking the child to Carmen's. Gathering up her things, his things, getting them out of the apartment on time, then over again the next day, the next week, the next month. Year after year. Carmen, close to seventy when Jonathan started kindergarten, would still walk over to the school to pick him up after Lidia dropped him off in the morning. He called her abuela-nana. The September he was five years old Jonathan could not speak a word of English. Carmen didn't own a t.v., so the child grew up listening to novelas and noticias on the radio, but by his first report card, Carmen had a difficult time getting him to speak to her in Spanish, so delighted he was to try out his new tongue. Lidia forced herself to teach him the alphabet in Spanish, before the English one was the only one he would ever know, though it required energy she didn't know she had left after too many years of two jobs.

Each night after the simple meals she had perfected, Lidia and Jonathan did their homework together on the floor, the only decent place to spread out paper and pencils, crayons and rulers. Her work entailed the cables and wires of buildings that were to jut out of the sandy soil of South Florida. His was of the life inside the buildings; whenever his mother botched a drawing, Jonathan took the discarded sheets to populate with uneven stick figures locked into the thickly delineated walls. He would adorn the frames on the outside with pygmy palm trees and mammoth tulips, the only flowers he knew how to draw although he had never seen a real one. His people, he told his mother, ate pizza

133

and papitas fritas, arroz con frijoles y hamburgers, like he did. And they spoke Spanish and English, he assured her; his own tongue swung easily between accented and unaccented English and a corrupted Spanish that amazed and delighted.

TWO FRIENDS AND THE SANTERA

"**WAIT A LITTLE** while I prepare the food, Estrellita. I've just come from la santera's." María drained then re-soaked some plump kidney beans in a pressure cooker while the other woman stood in the kitchen's doorway, watching. "Pobrecita, she is really in bad shape."

"Take your time, Mari." Estrella removed her short pale blue jacket. A plane approached Miami International near the Little Havana neighborhood, so she waited until she could hear herself speak. Since it was late afternoon and peak travel time, the women often had to wait for the planes to pass over. "What happened to Milagros? You saw her not too long ago, right? When she threw the coconut rinds for you."

"Ah, sí, you know she told me then that I definitely had to keep my promise to la Caridad del Cobre by a tribute of a fine white rooster. I left there so disconcerted. I thought about it a lot, but really, can you imagine?" María turned and noticed that Estrella was still standing. "Por favor, Estrella, sit. You're not going to make a doctor's visit, are you?

"Ya, ya. I'm sitting." Estrella chose the chair by the kitchen's sole window, next to the screen door leading to a fenced-in backyard. From her seat she could see two mockingbirds dancing in the grass behind the ground floor apartment.

Satisfied, María resumed spicing the thin minute steaks; the smells of onions and ground black pepper moved about the room depending on the breeze. "You know, I used to see mamá wring the necks of the chickens but this way they cut off the heads and pour the blood. Ay! I decided that I just couldn't do it so I went to see her today and asked her to ask the saints if a porcelain one were good enough. She had to ask them three times to make sure, but they said it would be all right. I saw a gorgeous white one at the botánica on Flagler last week. I have to take it to Milagros for Ochún's blessing." María twisted on the top of the espresso coffee pot and set it on the range. The gas pilot clicked several times before lighting; she adjusted the knob for a low flame. "The café will take a second—the milk's already warm. You have time, don't you?" She turned her head to look partly at her friend and partly out the window.

"And why not?" Estrella pulled her stocky legs out from under the table, arching thick ankles to release the tight shoes from her heels. "Ay, but the pace in this country is so fast. Hurry here, run there. We never seem to have a minute to ourselves but don't worry, mi amiga, for one of your cortaditos and a little conversation, always!" She sniffed at the aromatic café.

"You're so good," María said, smiling. "That's a pretty blouse. You didn't embroider that yourself?"

"But who do you think did it?"

"No?" María dried her hands before touching a mauve sleeve. "How beautiful." She rubbed the thin linen between her fingers.

"Isn't it though? This has its story too. I made about a dozen of these, all different colors, before I was married. I was lucky to get them all out of Cuba. I used different mother of pearl buttons for each one. You know, it's so true what they say about good things."

"Yes, I agree. Las cosas buenas siempre duran. They look almost new. Of course, we never had such luck of bringing anything here. Not that we had much." María pursed her lips.

"But you all were fortunate enough to get yourselves out of there when you did."

"Claro." An especially noisy plane flew very low. They could see from the window that it had propellers. María poured the black coffee into a demitasse cup and stirred in some sugar with a miniature spoon. She placed it before Estrella. "It's still very hot, be careful."

"Mmm, gracias. I like it like this." Estrella let the steam fill her nostrils before sipping it. "And the children?"

María poured the rest into a tall ribbed glass and swirled the coffee around to cool it off. She leaned against the yellowed-Formica counter. "Magaly is studying with her cousin Dulce María in the library and Toñito is probably playing fútbol. They never stop here."

"I know, since Bertica got married I feel so alone in the house and you know, my son with his things. He has so many records and tapes. All he does is lock himself up in his room with that music. He really worries me." Estrella moved her head from side to side.

"I haven't seen him around at all. It's a shame he and Toñito don't get along." The heavy pressure cooker clanked when María moved it to a back burner and turned up the heat.

"Ay, mi'ja!" Estrella's eyes swung up and half around, coming to rest on the mop and broom leaning against a dark corner of the kitchen. "It hurts me to say it but I think he's a lost cause."

They were quiet a moment, then another plane passed. Afterward, Estrella said, "Tell me about Milagros."

"Ah, sí. Well, she had finished with me and I was paying her—by the way, before I forget, her neighbor started making cantinas, so if you want to try her, I think her name is Odalys, let me know. Milagros says she cooks deliciously. Anyway, that's when she started to tell me what Ochún had asked of her. Niña, leave that cup alone! You remind me of my grandmother." María reached over.

"Ay, forgive me!" Estrella reluctantly gave up the cup and saucer but remained standing.

"I'll get it, sit down. Abuelita would always be taking things away from the table before a person was finished eating. You said you weren't in a hurry, no?"

"Yes, yes but you know I can't stand to be idle."

"Bueno, sit down and relax for once. There. You want water?" María took a dark plastic pitcher from the refrigerator.

"Sí, just a little. The café was good." Estrella wiped some perspiration from her forehead with a paper napkin. "Did I tell you that a man was killed right by my office today?"

"I heard something about it on the radio this afternoon. Dónde fue?" María pinned the thick springy hair back away from her ears. Steam was beginning to escape from the small metal valve on the pot's lid and the smell of peppers with it.

"Down the street near the fried chicken place. My supervisor saw them taking him away. It was right in the middle of the day. A young man. Stabbed. Probably a Marielito. I'm sure it had something to do with drugs."

"Qué cosa, qué Miami." María shook her head and sighed. A warm wind moved soft green banana leaves against the window from the outside and fluttered the religious calendar tacked to the wall within. She separated the white cotton blouse from her damp chest then undid the top button. The pressure cooker hissed fiercely until she covered the valve with its solid lead cap. The steam was then forced to hiss rhythmically, accompanying the women's talk.

"Calor, eh?" Estrella spread her legs a bit, pulling her skirt up some. "Loan me a nail file, Mari."

"Uh, hum." She found one in the drawer beneath the telephone. "Do you want me to paint them for you?"

"Ay, would you? I can never leave the little moons over the tops the way you do."

"Sure. Let me get the polishes. If you want, start taking that off." María brought out some cotton and acetone. She ran some warm water into a soapy dish then got her kit from the bedroom. Estrella began rubbing away the dark red from her nails.

"What were you telling me—before I interrupted you?

"De Milagros, chica." María laughed.

"Verdad que si." Estrella joined her.

María arranged emery boards, orange sticks and a cuticle cutter on a polish-dotted white towel. Estrella threw long strips of polish and acetone soaked cotton into the garbage, washed her hands, then returned and sat facing her friend, squaring her wide hips over the hard seat cushion. "Bueno, tell me about her troubles."

"Ochún has asked Milagros for her son to make the saint." María nodded for Estrella to put a hand into the water.

139

"No? But how is that?"

"He's to be initiated as a santero priest himself. She says that she's known it since he was very little because an old babalao in Cuba had told her about it. Her son is just about a man. A handsome boy. Shall I cut the cuticles back a bit?" María picked up the cuticle cutter.

"Sí, un poquito. Does he look like her?"

"He looks a lot like her. She showed me a picture. Fine features and shiny black, black, black skin."

"She has such a beautiful face. I remember her that time we went to that saint's celebration. If only she could lose a pound or two, but I should talk." Estrella shifted her thighs and moved down her skirt with an elbow. "Does she still wear her hair long?"

"Oh, yes, quite long and it's so thick. I asked her once if she had Indian ancestry, but she said all she knew of was some French blood. My father's sister married a French man, you know. They went to live in Europe when I was very little. Anyway, when Mariel happened, Milagros came here and remarried and all. She just didn't think about what the babalao had said. Imagínate; it was so long ago. Of course, you can't really forget something like that, and there was a time when she didn't have her instruments, that's what she calls them, her santera tools; she went for a long time without them. Then her son, Israel, started with all kinds of problems."

"Milagros has two little ones too, doesn't she?" Estrella's forehead creased a little.

"Another boy and a girl. They're less than a year apart and angels. You never hear them breathe when they're in the house. Just as obedient as I don't know what."

"And what happened with Israel?"

"Well, one time they were all in a terrible accident that totally destroyed their car. It was a big American car and she said big as it was, it was twisted like a rag. They had a blowout and her husband lost control and hit the wall on the expressway and flipped over a couple of times. They all got out without so much as a scratch except for the boy. His arm was crushed."

"The eldest son?" Estrella shifted in her seat.

"Yes. He was pinned inside and they had to use a machine to let him out."

"Pobrecito."

"That's not all. She said he had a long gash in his neck the shape of a machete an inch away from his jugular. Can you imagine?" María's eyes widened as she recounted.

"Mercy. These stories always frighten me." Estrella picked up a bottle of a dead rose polish but saw that it was lumpy and chose a bright red bottle instead that was almost full.

"This one's nice, isn't it? Magaly brought it for me." María shook it violently, clicking the little balls against the glass. "Milagros said that another time he was almost hit by a falling ceiling fan. He was sleeping under it on the sofa and she got a feeling that something was wrong or about to happen. She was at work so she called him and woke him up and that's when it fell."

"No!" Estrella's mouth opened wide. "Ay, María, look, my hairs are all standing up."

"Same thing happened to me when she told me about it." María shook her head without taking her eyes off of her friend's hand. "Poor woman. She says he's been getting into all sorts of trouble and she just doesn't know how she will raise so much money for the initiation."

"But how much does that cost? I don't know much about Santería but I never thought you had to pay for those things."

"Mi amiga, it has become like everything else in this country, a business. Milagros says that in Cuba people bartered whatever they had and used cash besides, but here all they want is money."

"Cuánto?" Estrella's voice lowered.

"She says it's anywhere from three to six thousand dollars."

"No? Que barbaridad!" Estrella shook her head to catch a breeze blowing through the kitchen.

"I couldn't believe it either. She's had to raise her fees. I used to pay her five dollars for the cocos and now she asks for any multiple of five because five's Ochún's number. I felt so bad for her, I gave her twenty, but would you believe, I had to force her to take it. She said, 'Más que basta con cinco y cinco.' But I wouldn't hear of it."

"Ay, I feel bad for her too, Mari. I really had no idea of the cost."

"Of course, don't you see all those exaggerated statues' shrines in front of the big houses?" María was thinking specifically about the Southwest area of Miami where many Cubans lived. A small shrine to Our Lady of Charity stood in the corner of the backyard surrounded by plastic daisies. Two planes passed one after the other.

"The babalaos make a lot of money whenever anyone makes the saint. You want the moon on the bottom of the nail too?" María asked.

"No, this is fine. I just like the top edges outlined in white.

My nails really aren't long enough for that. Your hands always look so good."

"Magaly is crazy to paint some designs on them."

"Ah, las muchachitas all love that." Estrella admired one finished hand. "You know, there's a guy who has a gas station on Le Jeune with an immense San Lázaro in front. Every year in December he makes a big party at his house. One time Bertica's friend, Kuki, knew a boy whose mother was helping to prepare the food so we all went. I never saw anything so splendid. They had one whole room dedicated to San Lázaro; his statue was surrounded by food for him. The entire floor was completely covered with the most beautiful fruit you'd ever want to see. There were mangoes of all colors, apples, and huge bunches of bananas hanging from the doorframes. Wine, grapes, oh, and lots of beans. They had plates of sesame candy and grain puddings. I'll never forget it."

"Those fiestas are really something." María looked up from her friend's hand a moment. "Estrella, I want to do something for Milagros. I told her I would sew the robes for Israel. She explained to me that she's not allowed to do it and she's such a fine seamstress too. The initiation preparation forbids her making his clothing or anything. Not even cutting his hair. She seemed very happy when I said I would help and then she wanted to give me back the money I had paid her. That would be bad luck but she was so excited she lost her head a minute."

"What has to be done?" Estrella shook both her hands in the air while María screwed the tops of bottles.

"Oh, it's beautiful work. She showed me a drawing for the robes she'd like for Israel; she said it was the same pattern as the ones she wore when she became a priestess. You know they have to burn them when the year is up? Seems a waste, but they use fine linen and silk anyway. It's part of the sacrifice, she says." María gathered up the files and orange sticks placing them in a large round tin, then returned the tin to her bedroom.

Estrella picked up the dish with the palms of her hands but María caught her as she dumped the water in the sink.

"You're going to mess up your nails. Sit down." She lowered the flame on the frijoles some more after pointing Estrella back to her chair.

"You know, Mari, I could help you. With the sewing, I mean. My machine is pretty fast."

"Ay, gracias, mi amiga. But I wouldn't want to put you through any trouble. It's just that I feel like I should do something for her. She's so sweet."

"I don't mind. Do you think it'll be all right with her?"

"I'm sure. I don't see why not. As long as she doesn't touch the materials." María paused a moment as the front door lock clicked and the hinges complained. "There's Magaly now. I need some rice and galletas from the market. Do you want her to get anything for you?"

"Ah, yes. I'd like some of those crackers too. They're better than the ones they sell at the bodeguita near my house." Estrella smiled up at her friend's teenage daughter just walking into the kitchen. "Hola, muchachita."

"Hello; eh, cómo estás?" Magaly touched Estrella's shoulder after putting her books down on the table. "Ugh, it's so hot. I can't wait to change."

"Well, don't get naked yet. I need you to go to the store for me."

"Ay, but Mami!" Magaly rolled her dark eyes. "I just got

here."

"You're young. You can walk. Where'd you leave your cousin?" María stroked her daughter's hair away from her face, almost as crinkly as her own.

"Dulce took the bus back to Miami Beach. She had a lot of homework to do but I think she might be coming over this weekend."

"Here, Magaly." María had taken out some dollar bills from her purse on the sofa in the adjoining room. "Leave that, Estrella, for god's sake, it's only fifty cents."

Using her palms, Estrella took up her own purse. "Take a dollar from the little zippered pocket, niña. Buy yourself a soda to cool off."

"Gracias. I'll be right back." Magaly turned toward the front door.

"Magaly." María spoke to her daughter's soaked back.

"Qué?" The girl pivoted around causing her ponytail to hit her face.

"Boba, you don't even know what I need!" The women laughed together.

Magaly tilted her head. "I forgot."

"What a child. I haven't told you Magaly." Estrella was still chuckling.

"Well?" A bright blush painted her cheeks.

"Get me some rice. This is the brand I want, o'kay?" María held up an empty rice bag from the trash. "Also, get two packages of the big Cuban crackers. And hurry back. I need the rice for today."

"Yes, Mami. Bye Estrella, let me kiss you in case you leave."

"No, mamita, I'll be waiting for my galletas."

"Ah, bueno, I'll kiss you anyway and then again later."

Estrella raised her wide chin. "Hasta luego, mi amor." The girl opened the front door while the women smiled behind her. "She's so affectionate, María."

"I don't know where she got it because I'm not like that. Her father likes to dote on her though."

"That's good." Estrella looked down at the large Cuban tiles that cooled her stockinged feet. "López has always been so, so, I don't know, indifferent?"

"No two people are the same. My mother used to tell me that her mother was very cold with them but to me and my sister, her grandchildren, she couldn't do enough."

"I never wanted to spoil the children, but still when they kiss me, it's seems a wonder. Bertica comes over often enough but you know, it's not the same. Leandro's shut up in his room all the time, I never see his face. And López, I don't have to tell you."

"Well, you never know." María moved away from the window to sit in the chair across from Estrella. "Maybe when Bertica has a baby, López will turn around."

"Ay, mi amiga, don't make me a grandmother yet!" They smiled into each other's face.

"As if I could stop time from passing. Who knows what's in store. By the way, you really should go with me the next time I see Milagros."

"I'm almost afraid to." Estrella bit her lip while María moved an unruly lock of hair away from her forehead. "My mother's family never talked about Santería although I think one of my father's uncles was a believer. My grandmother called it brujería. You know, vulgar; she didn't want anything to do with it. Myself," she sighed deeply and her bosom stretched her blouse, "I've never been to a santero."

"You don't have to have your fortune read or anything. I mean, it'll be a visit. Just to see her about the robes and all. You sure you want to help?"

"Oh, yes, yes. Poor woman. I'd like to help too . . . It's just that I really don't believe in those things, María, but I respect them."

"Ah, don't worry, Estrellita. Milagros will be very happy to know you."

MY DEAD

THAT FIRST SUMMER of my exile, I swept all the cuttings from around the beauticians' chairs and loaded and unloaded towels from the washer to the dryer, then folded and stored them away. Lelia, "la argentina," my mother's best friend, taught me how to scrub the brushes, wash the combs and soak the scissors in the blue liquid at each station.

Sometimes I sat at the receptionist's desk, answering the phones and scheduling appointments for Alan and Lelia. Billie liked to make her own appointments and leaned over me to take her calls—to her, everyone was darlin', honeychild or shuga. She sounded like some of the girls I knew back home. Her funkiness made me miss black folks. There weren't any in Lelia's neighborhood, but there weren't any kids hanging out either. I knew all along that I would miss a lot, but there was even more I never thought I would: There weren't any sidewalks but everyone had a driveway; there weren't any candy stores but gas stations were open all night. There were no stoops to monopolize, no fire escapes, no basements, no Main Street, no place to go or do anything and no one to do it with.

No one saw me cry because I didn't; I was kept busy at the salon. Soon I was handling the cash, taking the checks, giving change, walking over to the bank to make deposits. Lelia paid me a dollar an hour even though mami didn't want her to.

"Lelia, por favor, we're staying in your house, you've helped us so much," mami tried unsuccessfully to change her mind.

"Che, leave me. Gina is working hard for that money; she's helping me in my business," Lelia nodded toward me, "You leave us to our work."

I liked how she said it, our work, like I was more than some punk. I asked her if she would teach me to wash heads.

"Claro, of course, you can earn tips, sometimes a lot if you do a good job. One woman gave me five dollars one time because she liked the way I massaged her scalp."

Lelia had me do all her clients when she saw how careful I was with the blue and purple-haired ladies. Sometimes I had to help them lift their frail necks and heads from the bowl. But I was unprepared for the first time I saw the numbers on their arms. These tattoos were nothing like those of the roughnecks I'd seen.

One day I had finished rinsing out all the shampoo from the fine strands of hair and the sprayer misfired, landing water drops all over her forearm.

"I'm so sorry, Mrs. Fargas. Please forgive me," I grabbed a towel and began to wipe.

"Don't worry about it, sweetheart. It's nothing," she smiled and raised her upper body from the inclined chair.

I pushed back her sleeve and hesitated when I saw it. It was only a second but it was enough to change her expression. She cleared her throat and didn't meet my eyes again, not even when she gave me a tip or when she paid her bill.

Lelia saw the change in Mrs. Fargas and in me, but I knew

better than to ask about it in English. Later, between clients, Lelia asked me to come in the back room with her.

"That's a tattoo from the war, niña. That lady survived the Nazis." Lelia spoke quietly, addressing me in Spanish. "She was in a concentration camp, lots of these viejitas were. Those bastards marked them with numbers. Millions were assassinated, you know."

But I didn't know anything about holocausts, not yet. Soon I would be attending school with those ladies' grandchildren, who knew even less than I did.

Saying goodbye to friends and classmates was easier than I expected. At the end of every school year, everyone in the eighth grade, boys and girls, exchanged autograph books after graduation.

"What school are you going to?" Paulie asked as he folded back the corners of the yellow page he'd selected for his graffiti mark and message.

"I don't know." I hadn't even thought of it.

"Probably Miami High School, right?" Charlene entered the conversation; she had already doodled hearts all over the pink page she had dedicated to me.

"Naw. We're moving to Miami Beach."

"OK, Miami Beach High School," Paulie said as he wrote down the initials. "I know you are gonna have fun down there."

"Sure, she is. There are some superfine hunks in Miami," Charlene laughed and winked at me.

I didn't know anyone who lived there except for Lelia and her son, Ignacio and his bushy eyebrows and thick black arm hair made me remember his handsome brother and how he wasn't so lucky. And I didn't really want to think about boys either; the one I liked for the past year had asked Ivette out and they were going steady.

I thought of a way to turn this to my interests.

"I can get my driver's license in Florida when I'm fifteen."

"No shit?" Paulie looked up from his design.

"Damn! Lucky!" Charlene shoved me a little.

Paulie was already fifteen, starting high school later because he'd been left back. "Why do we have to be seventeen here? It sucks a big one."

"I'm going to work and save money for a car." Already a plan formed in my head.

Most of the farewell conversations went like that; no emotional outbursts, we were too cool. Three or four of the girls, not even my closest friends, asked that I write to them so we could become pen pals. But I didn't have an address anymore. The Galician family who bought our house had already taken over the first floor and was filling the basement with their things. Mami and papi gave away or sold most of our furniture; the rest was already on a truck heading south. I was happy that we were not taking the painted-over baby dresser or the battered bunk beds that my brother and I shared. Sick of the avocado green paneled kitchen with matching fridge and stove, I didn't care that we'd all have to sleep in one room at Lelia's house until we found our own.

On the trip from Jersey down to Miami, papi drove the newly purchased van filled with mami's houseplants and his tools while Mami drove the station wagon with us sleeping most of the way on the extended back part, blankets and pillows cushioning the bumps. We arrived in South Florida late at night but the smell woke me right up. I remembered it from every vacation—thick, ripe and green, like peppers and spring leaves.

Usually my family stayed for a whole month during the time when many Jersey factories laid off workers who then flocked to cheap and plentiful hotels in dilapidated South Beach. The southern end of Collins Avenue would be transformed into a Union City/West New York/Cuban enclave all summer. My friends and I would swim in every hotel pool from the Shore Club on 19th down to the Saint Moritz just below Lincoln Road. That was when all of Ocean Drive was populated by old folks on folding chairs, eyes fixed on the horizon as if waiting for an invasion. The mansion that would later become Versace's was boarded up, prohibiting trespassers from glimpsing at it except for the determined few who climbed to the roof of the hotel next door to look down at the trash-strewn courtyards and elegant steps. There were no hotels on the water again until 5th Street and they were too far to bother with.

But one summer was different. Mami and Lelia decided to go on vacation to Miami with just my brother, Gerardito, and me. Lelia's younger son, Ignacio, was too old to accompany us and working after school now; Amado had been in Vietnam for six months already, fighting for a country that hadn't granted him or his family citizenship yet. Our fathers, Amado's, and mine, were best friends too, but they couldn't take off from work since they had just opened the mechanic shop together. We were used to going to Florida every summer, but Lelia had never been. How they presented the idea of this trip to the men is lost to memory, but I imagine it was not highly calculated nor seen as scandalous or dangerous, even though their English together wasn't as fluent as one of us kids alone. Lelia's che-che-che-Spanish enchanted me. I hoped she never learned English, but I guess my brother and I were the insurance—translators, in case they couldn't make themselves understood because of their thick accents. As if I could help decipher what some southerner had to say. My brother's Spanish was getting sketchier by the minute. There was bound to be miscommunication.

We set out on our road trip, but I didn't think of our vacation as a road trip then in the way Americans do now. It was just the way our family traveled to Florida every summer—pile into the station wagon and spend two days fussing and annoying the hell out of each other, sweating in a fast moving car with overheated air rushing in through the open windows. We left northeastern New Jersey early in the morning, a bright, clear day, and took the ferry from Cape May and then the bridge over the Chesapeake. I think we had stopped for lunch somewhere along a quiet road—they decided against the turnpike and I-95 for the first part of the way, opting for the scenic route—and I remember picnic tables and shady trees and the women chirping, giggling, acting younger than me.

We ate the ham and cheese sandwiches mami packed. They had to economize; we'd have to stay in a motel overnight and then for ten days in Miami Beach. Lelia took the wheel after lunch and I remember staring at the straight, deserted road, uninteresting except for an occasional patch of woods and the dry ditch all along the right side. Mami was studying the map and I think Gerardito was sleeping. The novel I had purchased just for the trip, a comedic farce on the mob, lay unopened on my lap—I hadn't developed the habit of reading yet even though the silly cover attracted me. All of a sudden, there was an explosion and Lelia lost control of the car. Did it flip or just spin? I only remember being bumped about in the big sedan, papi's latest fixed up prize jalopy. I don't remember any screams or the time it took to stop, only, just as suddenly, quiet and much dust.

We ended up wedged in the ditch. We must have all been dazed, because even my brother the crybaby didn't cry. It took hours for us to get out of there and to a motel and then to get in contact with papi and Lorenzo, Lelia's husband. They drove down immediately, five hours, speeding all the way. They tried to see about fixing the car themselves but after a day of struggling, they sold it for junk; another day out of work could not pass so they dropped us at the bus depot, sent us on our way to Miami and returned to Jersey.

We arrived in sunny, moist Miami Beach sooner than if we had driven ourselves all the way. My mother and Lelia chose a hotel on Collins well below the condo canyon of North Beach. We had two spacious rooms with fancy curtains and lamps; there was even a sofa—nothing like the tacky rooms of previous summers. We went down to the beach, the water a shockingly aquamarine, then spent the day trying to forget the accident, the fright, trying to unwind. Mami and Lelia sat under an umbrella talking. When we got back to the room and had washed up for dinner, we got the news. I remember that we quickly repacked our things and returned to New Jersey on an airplane. When we got home, mami told me, but not my brother, that Amado was dead.

"Poor boy, may God forgive him. He killed himself." Mami crossed herself and closed her eyes in prayer.

"But why? How?" I asked, trying not to sound impertinent. I was going on thirteen; he was gone at eighteen. "Que paso?"

"Hija, you know Amado was such a good boy, so sweet and considerate of his mamá. The war was too ugly, too hard. He couldn't take it."

"But he wrote. He said he was ok." I thought this track might lead to the answer.

"No, mija, no. He told his mamá he was all right, but Lelia showed me his last letters and you could see he wasn't." She slowly shook her head and then just stared off.

I tried asking again but mami wiped her eyes and set her chin.

I realized I would have to ask my father who never measured his words like mami. Papi told me that Amado had hanged himself in Cambodia, behind enemy lines, in a country America kept denying we were in. He said that Amado wrote about children killed, entire villages burned. Papi said what Amado saw made him lose his mind.

It would take days for the body to be returned. Those were empty days, no playing, no music, no going over to my friend's. We were guardando luto, mourning Latin-style, which meant that even though it was the beginning of summer vacation and kids were out in the streets or at the park and exploding with energy, my brother and I sat as quietly as we could in Lelia's living room, fixed on the television but listening to her wails and Lorenzo's sobs. Ignacio, the remaining son, neither handsome nor sweet, was even quieter than we were. He made himself invisible in their tiny two-bedroom apartment. They had a window air conditioner that drowned out the grownups' limited conversations. Mami helped with the arrangements; her English was the most competent. She could read and write it while the other adults could not.

After a week, Amado's body arrived. The viewing was at one of the grand funeral homes along the boulevard. Our town, a small city with a village mentality, turned out. Amado was the first loss of the war on our block and my first funeral. Every family in the neighborhood came, not just the Latin, Caribbean and Central Americans but also the Italian, Irish, Polish and African American families. It was so strange to see them altogether; all dressed so formally, everyone serious. I didn't have a black dress, as mami considered it inappropriate for young girls to wear dark clothes, but I did have an almost navy blue dress with a wide white collar, buttons all the way down to my knees. Gerardito, who was three years younger, was excluded from the wake, though he went to the funeral; mami had to buy him a jacket since he had long outgrown his Easter suit. My three closest friends had come to the funeral parlor with their families; together with other neighbors, there were probably a dozen or more of us kids there. A group of them hovered over me and I knew I couldn't smile or laugh even though I was so glad to see them.

"I'm so sorry."

"Me too."

"Sorry for your loss."

Before I could respond, Lisa, Cindia and Ivette hugged me and then abruptly moved off together, leaving me alone in the front row. The boys didn't come near. They stood just inside the room and managed eye contact with nods. Tall flower arrangements crowded the walls and adults talked in hushed tones. My friends didn't really know Lelia, though their mothers did.

She set, combed, curled or dyed their hair in her kitchen in the evenings. They knew Amado even less since he never hung out around the block; he'd shipped out before graduation, before making any best friends among the older boys. I was sure they all probably knew the whole story by now and understood the shame involved with the sin of suicide. But what could they or I or even Amado know of war?

Amado wasn't my dead, but the situation led to my ownership of it. When I saw that there was an opening at the line before the flag-draped coffin, I approached. I had never seen a corpse before—my grandfathers died in Cuba before I was born and no one in the family had died here yet. What I saw was a smiling Amado, his crisp uniform more shocking than his gentle face. I knew that the scarf above his collar was to hide the rope burn.

Lelia was transformed from the funny, gregarious woman to a shell of grief, deflated, unable to stand by herself and, even more troubling to me, blankly silent. If Amado could see his mother then, I imagined he would have surrounded her with his arms, dropped to her feet, clasping her legs, saying over and over, *don't worry, mama, don't worry*. He had written her letters from a hell that neither she nor he could ever have imagined; his moral compass irrevocably scrambled, he tried but failed to take it like a man. *I'll be home soon, mother, I bought you a German cuckoo clock, wait till you see how beautiful.*

I didn't dare touch Amado's face, though earlier I saw Lelia stroking it and later Lorenzo kissing his son's clear forehead and cheeks. Standing over him, I could feel cool air emanating from the casket and I must have moved after a short while. I don't remember if I kneeled and prayed or just rudely stared. Many people came through the cold room. The Spanish-speakers said their *pésames*, the Latin way of extending sympathy; *I feel it* or *I feel it so much* not we're sorry. I wasn't allowed to stay there until closing; a neighbor took me home while mami and papi remained behind. In the morning was the mass at Our Lady Star of the Sea. That's where we went, because Lelia wasn't really a practicing Catholic—she reserved her Sunday mornings for laundry and cooking since the rest of the week was split between working days at the factory and doing hair at night.

There was a long line of cars, stretching almost ten blocks. The cemetery was in the midst of an industrial area, off a truck route in Jersey City. I remember there were several soldiers with rifles, a bugler and everyone strained to hear the priest over the rattle of passing trucks and cars. Shots were fired to memorialize and honor our offering. The flag was neatly folded and handed to Lelia who placed it on her lap and stared at it. His coffin was lowered into the ground and then there were more empty days to follow.

Summer dragged. By the time I was allowed to go out again, kids from the block treated me differently, like I was infected with something—bad luck or death. For the first time, I couldn't wait until school started.

A few months later, Lelia decided to leave the philandering Lorenzo, one of the things she admitted to herself after Amado's death. She took the insurance money, packed up her sorrow, gathered Ignacio, not a shadow of his brother, but alive, and bought a house in a Miami suburb. She rented a space in a strip mall and opened D'Amado's Beauty Salon. She'd call mami every weekend and rave about how beautiful it was, how many fruit trees there were everywhere, how cheap the houses were. We were in the middle of a winter without snow but the iciest in memory.

Mami seemed distracted after Lelia left. She and papi started talking nights after my brother and I were supposed to be asleep but I could hear them very clearly despite the frigid wind buffeting the storm windows.

"Lorenzo already has his puta living there ..." Mami was pushing but for what I couldn't tell.

"That's not the best of it. She's pregnant. " Papi added with a chuckle at the end.

"No! What shamelessness! The divorce hasn't been final not two months." She sucked her teeth.

"Really, it's getting hard to work with him all the time running upstairs to her and I'm alone in the shop. We made less last month than the month before and so far this month is the worst yet."

"Ay, and this weather has really agitated my bursitis. What are we going to do, Gerardo? Do you want start over?"

"I think so. We always thought we'd end up going someday, verdad?"

"Sí, y la niña finishes her last year and she could start secondary new. Dito will adjust, I'm sure of it. I think this might be the best time."

"Let's do it, vámonos."

Mami didn't the have guts to say so herself; she had papi sit us down to talk. I already knew what was coming. They had put up the house for sale the day before and when the kids in the neighborhood saw the sign and asked where I was moving to, I said Miami.

"After school ends this year we're going to la Florida but this time we're going to stay. You can feel like you are on vacation all year," she said smiling. Papi reached over to mess my brother's hair when he exclaimed in joy. I just sat there.

"We're going to buy a house with a big yard so you can have a dog," papi said while Gerardito jumped around in his chair. "And, you'll have your own rooms."

"Gina, do you have anything to say?" mami asked.

I didn't. A dog or my own room couldn't take the place of going to high school with all of my friends, even if they were still acting weird around me. Whenever mami didn't know how she felt about something, she'd say, she was neither cold nor hot about it. That's how I felt, neither cold nor hot. I calculated dates in my head: school finished June 20; Cindia's family was always in Miami for the 4th of July. Would we be there by then? Would I get to have new furniture? The stereo they promised me for graduation? Mami was still talking it up but I only half-listened.

"I know it's a lot to absorb but this is the right time to go. You love the beach and we can go all year. Lelia said she went swimming in December. Can you imagine? She said she hasn't needed a coat or sweater since she got there."

Then papi said something that perked up my ears.

"You know that you can drive in Florida with only 15 years?"

"Gerardo! Don't put ideas in her head," mami nervously eyed him.

Too late. I was imagining myself driving down Collins in my own car, taking my friends anywhere they wanted to go.

Lelia had settled in Skylake, a retiree suburb northwest of Miami Beach. Within two weeks of our move, papi found a warehouse district close by and set up his own mechanic shop. Mami was collecting unemployment and spent her days looking at houses while my brother watched t.v. and I worked with Lelia because I wasn't interested in cartoons anymore and the impeachment trials were on every other channel. But mostly because I couldn't stand myself any more than I could the relentless humidity and heat. I was glad to get out of the crowded house, to go to work at 7:30 every morning and return after sunset every night. We'd be inside in a dark corner of the mall, away from the bright, pounding sun, a relief.

D'Amado's Beauty Salon had six chairs but only three beauticians worked there—Lelia, Billie and Alan. Billie was my favorite because she was always teasing the ladies she worked on and she wore outrageously tight or low-cut outfits and a different colored wig every day. Alan was only a little more serious, but both of them seemed to be the right medicine for Lelia because she was back to being the fun woman who was my mother's best friend. She knew going in that most of her "bread-and-butter" clients would be the old women who shuffled or walked from one of the nearby condominiums or were dropped off by even older husbands. Alan and Billie wanted to attract younger women by hanging posters of the newest hairstyles throughout the salon and in the front windows, but Lelia was comfortable with her clientele; she affectionately called them her viejitas, her little old ladies. Sometimes their accents were as thick as hers, but theirs were Eastern European. I had never been around so many old people day after day. I couldn't imagine being their age or even my mother's age for that matter. I couldn't imagine what they had seen.

The only time I saw Lelia's face become drawn and still was when one of the viejitas asked about the handsome soldier's photo next to her mirror. We all paused. Lelia looked down at the lady's scalp as the rest of us gazed at Amado's tender smile in the black and white army portrait compelling us to silence. Lelia only said, "My son; he died in the war." After this, Billie or Alan would usually rush in to change the subject and I too learned the routine before long.

BEAST OF BuRDEN

FITO PuLLS ONTO the job site at 5:50 in the morning and the Mexicans are already there. Eight of them, all related, short, genial and they work like animals. It can be said he worked them like animals since he was the supervisor. The construction manager, José, only promoted Cubans since he could be assured they were legal, but Fito knew that wasn't the truth. He saw how they were treated; in solidarity, he tried to keep up with them and share the load. For the last week, it was the extra long sheetrock—all these new big houses had exaggeratedly high ceilings. It astonished him to see Benito pick up a couple by himself; Fito, a foot taller, skinny but who always thought himself strong, staggered when he tried. This family is from Zacatecas. He had no idea where that was, having never been anywhere but Cuba and here.

"Buenos días, muchachos," he called out as he slammed the truck door.

Several responded with smiles and nodding heads; the eldest, Rogelio, shook Fito's hand.

They all know the drill so they get right to it to beat the heaviest heat of the day. The construction manager will stop by between 10:00 and 10:30 a.m. and as soon as he leaves, they break for lunch. Every morning Fito remembers to always refill the cooler with fresh water and ice; none of them ever buy anything from the Dominican's lunch truck, not even sodas. He thought that maybe the aromas of frijoles, rice, carne guisada and other Caribbean dishes don't tempt them since these aren't spiced like their food.

Fito had never known any Mexicans in Cuba; he didn't get to travel much on the island and, of course, the tourist zones were heavily guarded. Since he didn't have a job in the tourism sector, he had no justification for being where foreigners would frequent. He had seen Mexican telenovelas, but none of them featured men like these men, all indigenous looking, stocky, without vanity. The dandies on the t.v. spent much time in front of mirrors, combing their shiny black hair and ordering their mustache. His co-workers, for this is how he thought of them, Rogelio, Benito, Manuel, Pancho, Octavio, Pablo, Jaime, and Julio Antonio, cooperated; it was an impressive thing. It's not like he didn't know about teamwork or the common good for he had done his duty as a youth cutting cane in the 10 million ton fiasco and showed as much effort as tolerated by others at the electric plant on the outskirts of Luyanó—since everyone got paid the same amount of money, irregardless of merit or productivity.

Fito didn't even "need" this job; it was a point of contention between him and his sister, Damarys.

"Fito, you can make as much money as you want if you take up Misael's part. I hate to just let it go. There would be no need for you to work like a dog in construction." She ran some figures by him; it was tempting but, for those figures Misael was now doing five to eight years somewhere up north.

"Hermana, I just want to know that you and the girls will be all right. If you need me to, I will work the business on the side to help out but . . ." Fito covered the papers in her hands with his hands. "Just tell me if you need me."

"I can't tell you that. The money is not a problem. You know that all the money won't bring Mima back or get Misael out sooner." His strong sister's lip quivered. "I don't want you to do anything that you don't want to. That's why we came to this country, verdad?"

He wasn't sure if that was true. Once his sister took his mother out of Cuba, Fito was left alone. His wife Gabriela had her family and their son, but he was the interloper in that household of too many people wishing he'd do more. A few more scrapes with the police precipitating a broken arm convinced him it was time for him to go too. Damarys came through on her promise to bring Gabriela and Gogi. But after a few months of living all together in his sister's big house, a tinge of dissatisfaction seeped in. Reunions are always incomplete, he thought, someone is missing, someone is left behind, or is dead.

"Mira, Dari, you know I will continue to collect the rents from the Miami houses, it's not a problem. And if you want, I can take on some numbers."

"No, no, that's not necessary. I'll say it again. I just want you to be comfortable. That you all don't lack for anything."

They left it at that. He let her pay for Gogi's private school after she argued that even through secondary, it would still cost less than one of her girls'quinceañera celebrations. He let her give him Misael's truck, a new super cab monstrosity of a Ford; she let him sell it when gas got too expensive and he bought the little Toyota he loved. She made him keep the difference.

It was always like this with her; she wanted him to do something or to give him something and they negotiated until she pretty much got her way. But she was like that with everyone. His brother-in-law, Misael, was not whipped but he liked to say that he, "Recognized the wisdom of her decisions." He loved and missed him, his sister's second husband, a jovial but astute man. They were boyhood friends before they were in-laws; Damarys teased Misael about Fito being more his brother than hers. In a way, it was true. Fito was nothing like his big sister who always seemed to be hatching plans, inventing businesses. He and Misael were accommodating; she led and they obliged.

Then Mima died and Fito wanted to die too. His mother had been sick for a long time, even in Cuba, though not so bad there. She had endured so much and survived; the disease fooled them all but maybe it was Mima who fooled them, hiding her pains. In the end, he was utterly unprepared for her last breath. It followed so closely on the heels of Misael's sentencing; mourning became complicated, lengthened and exaggerated because he wasn't there. His strong and loving brother-in-law, taken away from them too, for a time at least.

He had no idea why Damarys chose that saint for him. He was not a hunter; in fact, he hated to harm any animal, though he had no qualms about eating them—as long as somebody else did the killing. For so many years he didn't even regularly eat meat; it was too hard to find or too expensive when available. But even after being here for almost seven years now, he was just as skinny as he was in Cuba. Most everyone here called him Flaco. At least Damarys still called him Fito, his childhood name. With Mima gone and Misael away, she was only one who remembered anything about his childhood. Maybe that was the only difference that mattered here—the difference between living in Cuba where everybody knew everyone in the neighborhood and here, where there is so much space, and freedom and privacy. How to explain the comfort of that intimacy, of never needing to explain? The missing tooth—everyone knew a police knocked it out when he was picked up for loitering in front of his own house. The scarred shoulder? Most could recount, in detail, the motorcycle accident he survived but his first brother-in-law did not. His reticence? Most let him be, or teased him. Here it was expected that all mind their own business. Damarys explained it this way: In this country, you do your own thing and no one asks anything.

"If you keep to yourself, you will have no problems," she justified waving off neighbors before anyone got too close. "Get inside your house and that way no one can bother you, nobody sees anything."

Shortly after he arrived in the U.S., Damarys asked him to join her in the practice of Santería. She had already become a priestess by making the saint of Obatalá, the highest orisha and most important of the seven powers.

"Mira, Fito, people pay us for their petitions to be pursued. They pay for our saints' protection. If you join us, you will be the seventh. We'll have the pantheon. We'll have more power, and, of course, more money."

In Cuba, he attended the neighborhood tambores, enjoying the music, chanting and dances but in a detached way since he never joined the participants. As a boy, he remembered his father's only comment on Santería was, "I don't believe, but I respect." Yet Mima always had some offering to her virgencita and Papi knew that whatever flowers or sweets he found for her would end up on the altar.

Fito did not feel strongly one way or another. "What santo quota do you have to fill with me?" he asked his sister.

She smiled broadly, "Anyone who looks at you can see that you are a son of Ochosi."

"Hermana, are you trying to tell me something?" he laughed, recalling only minor details of the "divine hunter" with the keenest eyesight and surest aim but how he was cursed somehow.

"No, chico, no. Ochosi is long and lean like you, with the sharpest vision. Como tu." He had to hand it to her; she was persuasive to a fault.

He took the oath, did the rituals, shaved his head, wore white for a year. By the time his purification period was over, Gabriela and Gogi were preparing to join him in Miami. He wore the colored beads inside his shirt and, once they arrived, he successfully begged off all the evening "meetings" with petitioners and patrons to make up for the three years he was apart from his wife and son.

Even though Gabriela had some relatives in Miami, it was understood that she and Gogi would come to live with him at his sister's large ranch house in Homestead. She seemed stunned by the furnishings almost as much as she was shocked at how much space there was still leftover in every single room. Room enough for Gogi to run around without bumping into anything. He remembers one day that she shouted at the boy when he tried to ride his new bike through the house.

"But mami, it's raining outside," Gogi whined.

"Leave him, hija. There's nothing he can break that can't

be replaced. That's the marvelous thing about this country," Damarys said smiling, but he knew Gabriela wouldn't like it.

"Absolutely not! Gregorio, put that away," Gabriela did not like nicknames and refused to acknowledge the one everyone else used for their son and no one called her Gabi.

That was the first time he saw a flash of resentment in her eye and he thinks Mima saw it too because she tried to intervene.

"Gabriela, it's my fault; I told him to do it. I wanted to see how long he could ride without falling. Verdad, mi vida?" Mima kissed the top of Gogi's head, whose eyes pleaded with Gabriela. "It's just that your abuela is a shameless old fool," she kissed him again.

They had all been living together for four uncomfortable months and in such comfort. He never expected her to speak to his mother in the way that she did.

" Look here, Amalia," she said, using his mother's formal first name that no one used, "I understand that you all want Gregorio to have things he's never had before but I won't raise my son to be a savage animal. He simply cannot run wild."

"Of course, of course," Mima replied quickly before Damarys stuck her spoon in it. "I am in complete agreement with you. I'm very sorry. Ay, it's just that he was bored and I was being mischievous. Forgive a fresh old woman, ok?"

Fito had managed to keep Damarys from adding anything else by putting his finger across her lips. She shot him a glance that made him understand just how annoyed she was with Gabriela's display of character. Gogi hugged his abuela and then his mother.

"I'm sorry, mami. I won't do it again."

"I know you won't, son. Go, put that away," Gabriela said firmly, then walked back into "their" room. Damarys had put a big flat screen on the wall across from the four-poster bed that was so high, Gabriela and Gogi needed steps to get in it. His son was so used to sleeping with her that Fito slept on the sofa under the t.v. In Cuba, they had to climb up to the roof of her parents' house when they wanted to make love because the boy was such a light sleeper. There was no need to commandeer a rooftop now with two empty bedrooms at their disposal, but after the first month or so, Gabriela told him she didn't want to use them anymore so as to not call attention to their couplings.

"But you are my wife. They don't care," he tried to reason with her.

"I don't feel comfortable. Those rooms are on either side of your mother's room. It's too embarrassing." And that was the end of that conversation.

There were other things that embarrassed Gabriela, like having her laundry washed together with that of the rest of the family's. Damarys consented to having her sister-in-law's things washed separately, but it clearly displeased her; more and more he could tell that she was mightily holding back on telling her exactly how she felt.

The day Gabriela came upon him helping Damarys clean the instruments and large ceramic pots of the santos in their special room, she crossed herself and walked briskly away.

"What's up with her?" Damarys asked.

"Nothing. She doesn't like the santero business," he said, but before that moment, she had never directly admitted it. Every time he had to address one of the "things" that bothered Gabriela, he felt like a list was being drawn up—a column for her, dedicated to irrefutable evidence of why they couldn't, shouldn't, stay at his sister's, and a column for him, feeble rebuttals to contradict her evidence. After Misael got shot when a deal went sour, Gabriela stepped up her campaign.

"Mira, Ofelio, I am so appreciative of your sister's efforts to get us here, and all she's done, but I think it's time we start working on establishing ourselves, on our own," she said. She only used his first name when she was acting submissive. "I don't want to live as a dependent on your sister. It's not fair. Already el niño will be going to school all day and I can work too. We need to get our own apartment."

He could see the story she was writing for them in her gaze. A story not unlike the one Damarys envisioned: Work hard and you can get whatever you want. Such a different approach to life than what he had known all his Cuban life. Work hard or not, either way, you don't get shit. You don't pay rent but you live in decaying, close quarters with all these relatives stuck together in a partitioned house that is the family's only asset—which can be taken if you got into trouble with the Party. And only the devoted believers were invited to join the Party; his father had been a member early on, but when his own mother needed medicine that couldn't be found anywhere in Havana, he began to question, something not easily tolerated. It irked his father to ask the Miami-Cuban cousin to send the drugs; he hated not being able to defend the socialist ideals and when the CDR— Committee for the Defense of the Revolution—leader learned of his transactions, his father fell out of favor and was closely watched thereafter. It was probably a good thing papi died before the first of the various "special periods," Fito thought.

"Ofelio? Fito, what do you say?"

"Que?" He wasn't really listening, revisiting, as he was now, the struggles left behind to be replaced by others. Gabriela tried to grasp his full attention by sniffling and fussing with a tissue. From the next room, they could hear Mima's hoots and Gogi's yelps—they had a habit of tickling each other until one of them pissed from laughing so hard. Another "thing" that Gabriela frowned upon. She sniffled louder causing him to turn away from the wall.

"Finally, what will you do?" It was clear to him now that she was already gone.

And that is how it happened. A few months after Damarys moved them all to the palace she had built on the outskirts of Fort Myers, Gabriela was packing. She left to live with a cousin in an empty duplex in Miami; there was a job waiting for her at a bodega on Bird Road. A piece of shit job, but it was her excuse to back up the main justification for going—Gogi was to attend the private boys' school run by the same order of priests as the one in Havana.

Damarys showed surprising restraint when he talked to her about it.

"Of course, that is the best thing for him. An excellent school. You see, mi hermano, in this country, even the poor, wretched like us can attend the elite schools. Gogi will have an excellent education. Maybe he can become a lawyer so he can help get his uncle out of jail."

He knew she was only partly kidding. These days, her all was Misael, who at the time, was waiting to learn which federal prison he'd be warehoused in for the next three years.

"Hermana, look at what I have to do. I will stay here and work during the week and go to Miami on the weekends."

"I am not throwing you out! You stay, come and go as you please. As long as I have a house, you do too."

"I know, I know." He saw her eyes shine and cupped her chin, raising it. "I won't leave, I promise. I'll stay until Misael comes home . . ."

"But, your wife, your son . . ."

"I'll see them every weekend; it won't be bad."

She already knew that it was bad enough. Despite the distance from one end of the house where Damarys' and Misael's master suite dominated, to the other side where another master-like suite for him and Gabriela was located, their discussions seemed to be broadcast through the air conditioning venting—they could not be called arguments since Gabriela hardly raised her voice and he did rarely as well.

It got so that every time Gabriela walked into a room, everyone stopped talking or acting naturally. Damarys was loath to cause any more friction and, even though she herself was a raw bundle of nerves, she made sure not to even accidentally offend her sister-in-law. Fito saw it all and felt it so much, but he couldn't say.

His poor mother, sick and getting sicker, had tried, yet another time, to alleviate the tension. It was a Sunday afternoon, when they were all together, relaxing on the huge screened in patio in the new house. Maybe it was the last time they were all there, he thought back. His nieces, Yarely and Solimar, were playing with Gogi in the pool; it had a waterfall with a grotto behind it where the girls took turns jumping out of when Gogi came down the slide. Their shrieks and laughter made him laugh and Mima smile widely; she was rocking the baby, Betty, who was gurgling saliva over her bloated chest. Gabriela, never much of a swimmer, was vigilantly watching the cousins, one—a new mother at nineteen and the other a new bride at seventeen— to make sure they were not too rough with Gogi.

Fito remembers Damarys making a huge pot of fried rice with sausage, Misael's favorite. The girls' young husbands were playing pool with Misael. He was watching everyone from the hammock strung from one queen palm to another, a pleasurable completeness filled him; occasionally, he'd swing off, get a cold beer and shuffle the CD changer until a particular song struck the right chord.

An old Celia Cruz song precipitated Mima getting up and dancing the length of the summer kitchen. It amazed him that even when her disease had asserted itself again and she was in pain, she pushed right through it. Damarys started singing along. Humming, Fito approached Gabriela but she saw his shadow from the corner of her eye and snapped all the way around to face him.

"Don't even think about it."

"Come on, chica. Don't be like that," he tried to coax her but she was firmly planted.

For the others, nothing new about her response had passed, but for him, it was decidedly and most finally a rejection. And he understood it not just about himself but also of his whole family.

Mima saw, heard and acted. Quickly, she handed Betty to Misael and headed toward Fito whose head started to sink into his flat chest.

"No, no, no, no! *I'm* the one who has to dance this song with my son," she said with her arms stretched out, shimmying her shoulders. "Azúcar!" she shouted and grabbed Fito's hand, pulling him away from Gabriela.

"You can keep him, Amalia," Gabriela called out, turning back to watching their son.

Mima heard —they all did, but only Mima knew she meant it.

Fito drew his mother close and she whispered into his ear as they swayed together.

"Don't pay her too much mind; she's still trying to adapt. It's so much. She'll come 'round."

But she didn't. She left him and didn't even let him bring Gogi back to see Mima when she was dying, saying it would traumatize him. Every excuse or complaint was an arrow to his already weakened heart. He worked long hours trying to forget.

Fito had to praise the Mexicans for their work ethic; the first to arrive and the last to leave, and never did they complain about the heat or lack of shade. He considered Americanos stupid for wanting them out of the country—who throws out the one who puts a roof over your head or food onto your table? On this job site and at his previous one, all the workers doing hard labor were either Mexicans or other recent arrivals from Central America or the Caribbean. Nobody spoke, or needed to speak, English. Fito liked to hear their different accents and learned new words all the time. Though he rarely joined in on their chatter during lunch or breaks, he was interested enough to smile or shake his head when appropriate. It kept his mind off all that weighed him down.

One day Octavio was talking about how lucky it was that his sister was marrying a Puerto Rican, practically automatic citizenship.

"She met him at the restaurant where she works; he fell in love with her long hair. Pues, it hangs all the way down to her nalgas," he laughed.

"Find yourself a Boricua, then," encouraged Pablo as Fito snapped back a tape measure from a molding.

"Jefe," Octavio turned to Fito saying, "do you have a sister or cousin who will marry me so I can get papers?"

His smile was both sad and resigned. "I have a wife you might try," he said, winking.

FORGED LIVES

ALREADY MARRIED WITH one daughter by the time los barbudos strode into Havana like they owned the world, or the world owed them, Eduardo was both disinterested and naturally skeptical of the revolutionary platform. From his perspective, as co-owner of a canning factory in Regla, anything that disrupted business was bad news. Who would pay him for the loss of four days when everyone went on strike? Even though he was an exemplary boss, working hard and side by side with his dozen or so employees, paying decent wages and all the canned fruit they could carry home on Fridays, they walked too.

"Sorry, jefe. We want to show solidarity," said Rafael as he gathered his things on his way out, "You know how it is."

"I understand," Eduardo had said, but he worried they might expect back wages and if the factory wasn't working, money wasn't coming in. He was thinking about his pregnant Luisa and their little Luisita when he thought he could manage to run a couple of machines by himself, but a minor miscalculation in timing led to the loss of two and a half fingers. Just weeks after the accident, he surprised all with his remarkably dexterous remaining digits. So he could still work, as hard or harder than he used to, and when his partner Álvaro said he was leaving for la yuma and asked him to buy out his share for a fraction of what was fair, Eduardo embraced the opportunity.

"Mi amigo, things here are going to get worse; that strike was only the beginning," said an unusually serious Álvaro; then he bit down on the end of a stubby cigar.

"It can't go on forever although I know what you are going to say . . . " Eduardo gestured toward his partner.

"There's no evil that can last 100 years," they chimed together and laughed.

"Look, it will settle down. It always does. We'll ride it out," Eduardo patted him on the shoulders, "Who knows, I may end up en el norte and we can start another business together, verdad?"

"I wish you'd make arrangements now, brother. There's so much chaos right now, you can move money without a problem," Álvaro sighed.

"Don't worry. We'll be all right. Whenever the government changes, business improves; people get optimistic. Look at all the flags! My neighbor's made a fortune selling them—she couldn't keep up with the demand." Eduardo willed himself to see the bright side. He was going to be full owner of the factory; he would have all the responsibility but all the profit too.

"Well, I hope for your sake that you're right. For my family, this is the right time to get out. Julia's parents are already in Miami waiting—they found a house and a school for the children. With this money," he fingered the check equaling his share of the business, "we'll be able to make a new start."

"You will become a captain of industry in el norte!" Eduardo teased him with their old standing joke about being exemplars among entrepreneurs. In truth, neither man had an exorbitant lifestyle. Yes, both of their coiffed wives played cards everyday at the club, and their children had nannies and cooks prepared their meals. Each man had decided, independently, to leave newer homes in their sprawling Havana suburbs to be closer to the factory and purchased big, old houses with heavy doors and window shutters, thick cooling walls and peaceful inner court-yards— all earned by their own labor since neither man had attended university nor inherited family wealth. They did not consider themselves rich, but merely comfortable.

No such comfort now, Eduardo thought to himself, remember-ing that it was the anniversary of the attack at the Moncado Barracks. Back in Cuba, all workers, all school children, all able bodies were forced to "celebrate" by marching to the Revolu-tionary Plaza, waving flags. But now, in the U.S., he didn't have to do anything but die. So much tumult in a lifetime, he wasn't one to question the cancer eating away at his insides now. Edu-ardo had heard of people wising up quickly when confronted with their mortality, but from his perspective, what was there to learn? He sat on the sheet-covered easy chair today like most days and every evening in his narrow Florida room in a small VA-era built house he shared with Luisa in Broward County. All day, every day and evening they watched Spanish language television—news, talk shows, novellas, and variety shows. During baseball season, Luisa excused herself and watched the little black and white set in their bedroom. Their only income was social security, so they sold their second car and did with-out long distance phone service and air conditioning during the days in order to keep the cable. Luisita brought groceries every couple of weeks and Elenita, bless her heart, sent a little check whenever she could. Old enough for Medicare, now poor enough for Medicaid, Edurardo had stopped working as a mechanic two years ago when the pains in his lower back prohibited him from looking under or over any engine. Luisa kept working until he could no longer take care of himself; he was utterly inept at changing the bag of nastiness made necessary by the now permanent colostomy after the second unsuccessful surgery. Eduardo's emphysema required oxygen—dragging the tank around effectively ended his predisposition to pensive pacing, the way he gathered his thoughts. He had to reorient himself to thinking while sitting. Each time he checked his blood sugar, he found that something about the pinprick, the blood drop and the numbers caused him to reminisce.

He prepared the syringe for his morning shot and began to fall into his usual reverie of memories, full of disillusions ending only occasionally in clarity. Luisa was washing the breakfast dishes and he thought to himself how his fortunes had turned out. Once a robust man, so strong, now surrounded by tubes, unable to even go on the toilet. Perhaps he was luckier than most since he had had two lives; his Cuban one was the longest and longest-suffering—sixty years. His American life, going on five years—if he survived the next brutal round of chemo—was the shortest and peppered with its own burdens.

He thought of his Cuban life. About the struggle, waiting, and despair. There was all the time in the world to think and no time at all. No one could really get over; getting by was considered the bounty of the revolution.

Álvaro got out before the presidency was dissolved, before the utilities companies were nationalized, before Playa Giron, before Luisa lost the second baby, a boy, the only one in a family still dominated by females. His partner was right after all; it was clearer every day that it was only a matter of time before he'd lose the factory. Eduardo started buying gold jewelry and sending it out of the country with friends who were able to leave— some off to Spain or Mexico. He considered sending Luisa and the girls ahead of him because he wouldn't leave until he had to, until they made him. Or let him.

Ten years after the revolution, everyone was being recruited to work in the spectacular disaster of the Ten Million Ton Harvest. Luisita was thirteen and already being ostracized for not spouting party slogans and refusing to wear the pioneers' neckties. He arranged for his doctor friend to document her fabricated mind-numbing migraines brought on by sun and heat; there was no way she could be sent to the countryside to cut cane but the cost was high. Luisita was refused enrollment to attend the academic secondary school, dashing her dreams of becoming a doctor. She despaired at the lack of challenge at the technical school, such an intelligent child as she was, but soon she learned to complete all her homework in class and in the evenings began attending rehearsals at the theatre near her school. She was volunteering as a line coach when it was clear that her memorization and delivery of lines was far superior to that of most seasoned actors', but she was cast in only minor roles—non-communists would never be allowed to lead.

Elenita was blessedly still too young for the harvest, but she already noticed the teachers' prejudice. She made it part of her daily routine to recite the catalog of offenses.

"Papá, I have three complaints to report today," she sat on his lap after slamming her books down on the table.

"Well, I can see you are indignant, so fire away."

"First, and this is the same one from everyday, Señorita García refuses to call on me even when I'm the first one to raise my hand," she started.

"But, hija, if this is a repeated offense, does it count?"

"Of course, Papá. Don't you see that each and every time, it must be reported?" She was so serious, so resolute; she'd make an outstanding lawyer if only they'd let her advance.

"Yes, of course, you are right, hija. Qué más?"

"Well, it just so happens that I got the highest grade on the weekly script test," she leaned over to retrieve the discolored, lined paper to show him, "See? But why do I have it here? Because that . . . ," she stopped, looked at his raised eyebrows and continued, "woman will not post my work."

"What a shame, my sky. It's very pretty." He nodded with his chin.

"Finally, and this is nothing against gorditos, papi," she squeezed his bulk, "but she moved my seat to be behind fat-frog-face José Bernardo, the most odious kid. He picks his nose and plasters the snot on others, he belches and farts and, papi, he smells like onions all the time." She wrinkled her nose.

"Bueno, hija, there is always going to be a José Bernardo. You have to learn how to cope."

How they had all learned to cope. That was every Cuban's modis operandi, regardless of their connections or lack thereof, and even when they thought it couldn't get any worse, the stakes were raised and the hole they were sunk in deepened. He wanted to believe that his hard work would safeguard him against confiscation of the factory, that his employees, his co-workers, wouldn't let Fidel take it over.

The early years of the Revolution were marked by a fierce nationalism that choked the squeamish. The Russian-dominated decades—tall impossibly pale technocrats invaded all segments of society; then there was the African honeymoon—when many injured Angolan soldiers came to Cuba to recuperate and children learned the capitals of every African country. Fidel went out of his way to embrace Cuban's African-ness when he was sending troops into Angola and Guinea-Bissau. It suited him to recognize the significance of Santería when he realized he could earn a profit for all the acolytes willing to travel to Cuba to be made high priests. In Eduardo's own Regla neighborhood across the bay from Havana, there was a santo-factory. It would not do well for the party to sacrifice animals in any of the more densely populated areas when people were eating broths with only a hint of fish or fowl.

Later, in the special periods, and even these Fidel admitted, were the "difficult times"—when glasnost and perestroika exploded the stinking and rotten foundation of the Cuban economy and all felt the next bottom hit—money from the ones who had left returned with their hopes and dreams of reunion, re-integration.

By 1979, Luisita announced she was going to marry a political prisoner in order to get the hell off the island. She had been systematically excluded from every venture she'd attempted. Eduardo was working along with Luisa in the factory, which was no longer his, and Elenita was finishing secondary at a school in another province. There was no way to extricate the politics from the academics—to study law, Elena'd have to disavow her parents' and sister's bourgeoisies tendencies. It broke her mother's heart to let her go, but it broke his own more to not let her follow her intellect.

Luisita's marriage to Saúl was questioned and ridiculed; the guards called him maricon and sent him to the faggot cell so that he would be "more comfortable." But after several months and an international delegation that happened to visit the prison where he was, the government gave them permission to leave the island. All of Saúl's stateside family was already waiting in Spain when they arrived. Luisita and Saúl would have to establish residence there until their American paperwork allowed them to come to the U.S.

Eduardo's sisters, Nena in Florida and Amalia in Marianoa, both encouraged him to go; Nena sent wires and money. Ama gave him the last of their mother's jewelry to sell. He and Luisa began giving away things, even before they knew they were leaving. Elenita noticed.

"Mamá? Papá?" she called out one day when coming home for the weekend. "Eh, where is the little marble table?" It was where everyone dropped keys or bags upon entering. "Oye, and what is this big box here by the door?"

He found her examining the good china Luisa had packed up to give to her cousin.

"Papá?" Her gaze bore through him. "Qué es esto?"

"Ah, that's your mother giving away all her good things. She's too generous." He tried miserably to cover up but Elenita wasn't having it.

"Papi, I don't want to leave. I'll be an adult soon; I have a chance to study at la universidad de la habana. It's not fair to me . . ."

How to tell her that her chances were already squashed? She didn't know the price she had paid and would continue to pay for her sister's freedom.

"My love, nothing in this godforsaken place is fair," he said brushing away hot tears from her flushed cheeks. He couldn't bear watching another child live through continuous disappointment and discouragement. By then, they learned their house would be confiscated and would mean a return to his failing mother's already crowded house. Eduardo's mother, Pilar, had doted on him as a child, her firstborn and only son. Never much of a playboy, she encouraged him to sow his oats; no woman could replace her, she schooled him, but then she rejected his choice for wife, rupturing their once unwavering bond.

His marriage to the lovely Luisa, the sweetest, most beautiful woman in his barrio, was celebrated by a notary at his mother's. In all the photos, Pilar's downturned gaze and dour expression contrasted with the others' shinning eyes and joy-filled faces. Luisa knew well how to comfort him and never, ever spoke ill of her mother-in-law though she had every right to do so; Pilar never let an opportunity pass without some complaint or puyita lodged her. But even as ridiculously petty and spiteful as she was to Luisa, what hurt him most was his mother's indifference to his girls. Praise God and all the santos, Luisita and Elenita were just like their mother—tall, lean, sweetness oozing from every smooth pore and elegant follicle. The girls knew not to expect any fawning or caresses when they visited Abuela Pilar and not surprisingly, they left off accompanying him as soon as they had "legitimate" excuses involving school.

Eduardo pushed the easy chair's handle back, extended his legs and pretended to doze so as to avoid any distractions. He remembered the last straw that landed when Elenita discovered a letter her grandmother had tucked inside a book she borrowed from a cousin. Addressed to no one, it was pure vitriol, cataloguing Luisa's poor character and personal offenses that no one could corroborate, for without question, confronting his mother was the first thing he did when a weepy Elenita presented him with the damp and wrinkled letter. Pilar's temper and appetite for drama were legendary; she fairly fainted before him and Amalia rushed in the room to apply an alcohol-soaked rag to her mother's face and neck.

"My son, my son . . . I will have to forget you. I cannot, I cannot . . . I cannot subject myself to such, such treatment," Pilar sobbed, beating her chest for emphasis. "Abusive treatment. Not even a dog deserves it. I cannot. I cannot."

The more she carried on, the steelier he became.

That time Eduardo left his mother's house and didn't return again until almost fifteen years later. In the interim, he drank excessively; this was not so extraordinary since like most everyone else in Cuba, what else does one fill his belly with when there was little food to be found? And he also smoked excessively, another way to keep his mind off the rift. Besides his work at the factory, of course, Luisa and his girls were his world.

"Eduardo? Eduardo, my life," Luisa was calling him. For a moment he couldn't remember if they were in his mother's house or in their own house. Was he in Cuba or in Florida?

"Edi, chico. Wake up. It's time to change it," she said, moving near him with her tray of supplies.

Eduardo was glad that she didn't mention the bag; he tried to put it out of his mind as much as possible. He was amazed that she could complete the process so quickly and without so much as an unpleasant odor. He wasn't disgusted by strong smells for he loved the stink of grease, diesel and oil—he was ashamed that she would have to smell it. As soon as she took it away, he extended his feet again and closed his eyes. This time he recalled their last months in Cuba when they had to live with his mother, sister and nieces in a house where he was once the favored son.

Their arrival was neither bittersweet nor remarkable, for there was no reconciliation. Amalia negotiated, as expected of the middle child, giving up her room for him, Luisa and Elenita.

"I'm happy to do whatever I can for your return home," she said, stroking Elenita's hair; her excessive fussing made them all uncomfortable.

Eduardo and Luisa had lived with them as newlyweds for a tense year when their new house was being built. Luisa refused to return to his mother's after Luisita was born, preferring to move—straight from the clinic—into the practically empty house blocks away.

This time Luisa spoke, addressing Amalia but loud enough for her mother-in-law to hear: "No, mi cuñada, this was never our home but we appreciate your sacrifice for us."

Pilar made a sound but Eduardo shifted his substantial weight and shot a sidelong look her way. She settled back in her invalid's chair and posture. Still the only man in a house of women, his broad shoulders and barrel chest remained imposing despite his thinning hair and lumbering gait. Subdued, Pilar stopped talking. A blessing Luisa thanked God for every single night of the sixty-seven days they stayed.

On one of those nights, Luisa spoke softly though firmly into the darkness—Elenita was watching a Venezuelan novela with her cousins in the front room.

"Eduardo, mi vida. You awake?"

"Sí, qué pasa?" he said turning to face her.

"You know what I'm going to say, don't you?"

He did but didn't offer anything except, "Tell me."

"You know we can't stay here. I feel bad for your sister, such a good soul but can't you see how even she is stressed to the limit? Do you see how it's affecting Elena?"

Eduardo saw it all. Elenita staying away all the livelong day, Luisa holed up in "their" room all evening, his sister trying to keep everyone from confrontation by making wine and blasting the television he brought from their home, a pack of restless teenage nieces endlessly bickering, and his mother who spent her time sucking her teeth or moaning whenever he was in earshot.

Beleaguered and fed up when a chance dropped from the heavens. The Peruvian Embassy's gates were crashed open. Frenetic excitement coursed through Havana, something even Fidel couldn't control. People walked, ran, drove by the embassy to confirm the wild rumors—that there were no guards! People murmured asylum, asylum, asylum. Then Fidel said whoever wants to go, should, and Eduardo sat Luisa down.

"Vámonos. Let's risk it. They say whoever gets on the embassy grounds will get safe conduct to leave," he said trembling. Luisita and Saúl were already settled in a Madrid flat, counting the days until they could emigrate to the US. Elenita was starting to get the cold shoulder from her school compañeras but still toed the party line irrespective of their treatment. Amalia wept continuously but gave him all the cash she had in the house and sold her bootleg wine to replenish her cache.

"Sister, this means so much to me, to us. A thousand thanks are insufficient," he held her heaving body.

"My brother, I only wish you all the best," she said stoically; their mother sat across the room and stared at them. Luisa had already said her goodbyes and was nervously waiting outside to get to the embassy. Eduardo decided to address his mother directly.

He pulled up a stool, lowering himself to her eye-level. She didn't blink her cloudy eyes, once a vivid green, and neither did he.

"Mima, we're leaving now." He paused, contemplating his next utterance. "I don't know that we will see each other again in this life." She moved her lips but made no reply.

"Adiós," he said after a lengthy pause, stood and gathered his things.

She said "God protect you" to his back; he did not turn around.

Eduardo deeply exhaled and opened his eyes. Luisa was smiling next to him. Her own easy chair also extended, covered with a sheet and damp with sweat.

"What a fine pair we make, eh?" She chuckled. "I was thinking that we will be married forty-five years come December. Can you believe it, Edi?"

Before he could answer, he felt a sudden tightness in his chest, the sharpness of which filled his eyes.

"My love, what's wrong?" She snapped her feet down and touched his clammy arm. "What's the matter?"

Eduardo shook his head, first softly then more vigorously, shaking tears from his face. Pain radiated from his chest to his head, from his arm to his throat; a razor had cut off his breath and a metallic taste coated his tongue. He was not afraid of dying; he was just expecting it to take him bit by bit, not all in one fell swoop.

With no time to think, Luisa whirled around him, shaking him, trying to keep his eyes focused, trying, trying…

AFTERWORD

AS BOTH OF my parents were born and raised in Cuba, I have long been moved by the plight of the Marielitos, the Cuban exiles who arrived in the United States via the 1980 Mariel boatlift. A large portion of these refugees settled in Miami, where, back in 1986, I was teaching high school remedial English to "minority" students (even though, ironically, the "minority" students were the majority population in both the school and the city). Seeing how Miami adapted and changed because of the presence of the Marielitos, I felt that someone had to write about these people, preferably someone who was one of them. Other writers, mainly North American Anglos, had written about these exiles, but I wanted to articulate the accents, intuitions and ritmos (rhythms) that I hadn't heard or seen before in print.

In February 1987, I wrote the first story in what would eventually grow into this collection, "A Matter of Opinion." The tale of a woman whose Marielito nephew is incarcerated without a trial, I submitted it, along with some earlier work, to the University at Albany's doctoral program in creative writing, where I was accepted in April of 1987.

During my first year at Albany, I wrote several other stories that would make their way into this collection, including "The Fresh Boys," a tribute to my former Miami high school students, and "La Buena Vida." Juan's story in "La Buena Vida" set me going on the next piece "El Loco." These two stories are connected because Juan's killer at the end of "La Buena Vida" is El Loco.

At the same time that I was working on these stories, something happened which changed the way that I thought about language in my work. I was browsing in a bookstore one day when I came upon an anthology called *Cuentos: Stories by Latinas*. The editors' introduction to the book clarified the conflicted feelings that I had been having for years about writing in both English and Spanish. Before that, no matter how hard I tried, I had never been able to reconcile the Spanish in my English and the English in my Spanish. After all, Spanish was my first language, the tongue spoken in my home while I was growing up. I had wrestled with this "problem" in my writing for a long time, until the editors of *Cuentos*—Alma Gómez, Cherríe Moraga, Marian Romo-Carmona and Myrtha Chabran—helped me to see how important, indeed, legitimate, my dual usage of language was. I was inspired that one of the purposes of their anthology was to ". . . help the reader become accustomed to seeing two languages in a book, learning to make sense of a thing by picking up snatches here, phrases there, listening and reading differently." After reading the introduction to *Cuentos*, for the first time I truly felt linguistically liberated, as if a great weight had been removed from my tired shoulders. At last, I had found the aesthetic context of my work.

Today, I consider myself a Latina writer. Spanish is sprinkled throughout my work as it is throughout my life. I write about my people for my people. I know the characters personally; they inhabit my head in the same way that the characters of *The Color Purple* inhabited Alice Walker's head. When I first read her essay "In Search of Our Mother's Gardens," it stirred me into sadness for the lack of models/gardens in my life—my mother had had no garden, only factory jobs for too many years. In searching for my mother's and ancestors' gardens, I began to research Cuban women writers and eventually found my own Zora Neale Hurston—Lydia Cabrera, a Cuban anthropologist, folklorist and writer. Her tales of black Cubans and of the saints/orishas—Yourba gods of the Afro-Cuban religion Santería—excited me into further research into the subject. The story "Two Friends and the Santera" stems from that research and reading, as well as "A Fraction of Always" and "Beast of Burden."

In addition to the writing and ideas of Cabrera, the stories of Flannery O'Connor are also favorites of mine—her characters, the tension she builds in such small places, and let's face it, no one knows how to title a story like she did. I also love the work of Toni Morrison, and find here and there similarities in the easiness of dialogue: An action by a character that is only witnessed by someone who intently though seemingly disinterestedly watches; a woman scratching her scalp; a man's morning erection; a baby sweating to death. One of the books that most haunts my life is Morrison's *Sula*. "La Buena Vida" begins with a joke, a Marielito joke—just as *Sula* opened with a joke, a nigger joke.

Although as a reader I have some problems with Julio Cortázar—his sexism and violence against women for instance—his experimentation with language greatly influenced the stories "Puyas" and to a lesser extent "La Pareja." I am intrigued with the complexity in the simplicity of his short stories, and was stylistically liberated by his prose in a way one's "load" in life is lightened when she discovers a shortcut to work that shaves fifteen minutes off the daily commute. Reading Cortázar, page after page of prose that is still one paragraph, sometimes one sentence, I decided it was time to move away from the conventional forms of my early writing training. The stories in this collection are far from unconventional, but for me to write the large sections of "Puyas" in exposition and avoid some perfectly good dialogue and action marked quite a move for me.

Finally, I feel the need to address the issue of gender. I am a feminist who happens to be a Cuban American woman writer; a Cuban American woman writer who happens to be a feminist. My politics inform my work and my reading of the stories. When I read/listen to the women talking in "Two Friends and the Santera" I feel that is a woman-centered story written in a form that reflects a woman's perception of what happens in that kitchen. Sometimes, I write stories that are man-centered in the way that "The Fresh Boys" is about three young men; it does not tell the story, really, of the women in their lives.

In addition, my feminism allows me to recognize the politics of a non-stance in writing about a people who fear communism more than anything. Marielitos are perhaps not as far right as the Cuban exiles who arrived in the United States in the 1960s and '70s, while the Balseros in this collection are even less interested in politics. Over the years, some people in "el norte" have referred to me as a fascist (since the characters in my collection leave socialist Cuba, this implies that the island is not paradise). At the same time, in Miami, some have taunted me with the name communist—how dare I imply that there is anything good about socialist Cuba (for example, Elena in "Forged Lives" would have stayed if she had her druthers and the "Fresh" boys didn't want to come to the U.S. either). In the end, I figure that I am doing all right if I make both leftists and rightists angry.

Ultimately, my feminism, as well as my background as a child of immigrants, spouse of a Cuban exile, and mother of two bilingual, bicultural children has allowed me the vision to see the necessity of sharing the stories of the exiles in this collection. At first I told these stories so that we, my people, wouldn't forget them. Now, given the unending and enormous difficulties that island Cubans face and the greedy desperation some mainland Cubans feel at the prospect of returning "home" to do "business," the stories serve as a warning of a disturbing rejection we impose amongst and against our own.

The stories here are generally connected by ethnicity, class and time (the 1980s through to the early 2000s), and it is my hope to give the reader some of the flavor of the Cuban American experience, though I know, ultimately, that it is my own experience and my interpretation of it. Because I know the stories, characters, habits, gestures, voices, and fears of the Cuban exile community, I hope that readers will come away from this collection with a powerful recognition of our shared humanity.

ACKNOWLEDGEMENTS

Gracias mami, papi, Daniel, Mabel, todo mi familia de sangre y corazón. To all of my dear and beloved friends and family—too numerous to single out one by one—a thousand heartfelt thanks for your tolerant humoring of my dream. Jorge, gracias for your pride in me and support all of these years. Ivonne Lamazares and Elena Pérez, grateful thanks for never failing to believe in me even when I stopped believing in myself; your unwavering encouragement helped me persevere. Iliana Jiménez and Yolanda Lamela (Illy and Yoly)—not just friends but sisters—through thick and thin, gracias por tu apoyo. Love and laughter from so many great friends like Lisa Roy-Davis, Grisette Acevedo, Litza Fonseca, Isabel Barrabeitg and Claire Mauer make life better. A special thank you to Janet Bohaç who has shared her writing/life with me in fortifying letters for almost thirty years.

To all of my wonderful teachers and mentors, Barbara McCaskill, Rita Deutsch, Gene Mirabelli, Gene Garber, Toni Morrison and many others whose example led me to a career in teaching and writing. To my classmates and colleagues, caring friends each and every one, all highly valued and admired: Michelle Barrial, MaryAnn Cain, Esperanza Cintrón, Kevin Meehan, Martha Marinara, Annabelle Conroy, M.C. Santana, Alma Negy, Maria de Jesús González, Victor Villanueva, Luis Martínez-Fernández, Ahimsa Bodhrán, Bobbi Ciriza Houtchens, MaryCarmen Cruz and more—your friendship and support sustained me in important ways.

Gracias a Dios y a todo los santos, especially Santa Barbara, La Caridad del Cobre, La Virgen de Guadalupe and the Infant of Prague, my own sweet baby Jesus.